# THE TIN GOD OF TWISTED RIVER

When Hashknife Hartley received a six-months-old anonymous letter warning him to stay away from Arapaho City, a place he had never heard of, his curiosity was aroused. So he and Sleepy Stevens set off for the Twisted River country to find out what it was all about. As they approached their journey's end they were shot at by an angry ranchman, Hank Ludden, in mistake for rustlers. But they survived, as usual, and joined the ranchers in tracking down the notoriously active rustlers . . .

# THE TIN GOD OF TWISTED RIVER

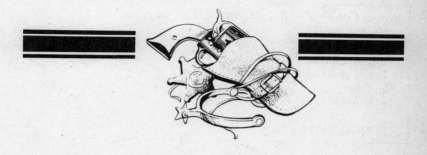

## W. C. Tuttle

ATLANTIC LARGE PRINT
Chivers Press, Bath, England.
John Curley & Associates Inc.,
South Yarmouth, Mass., USA.

Library of Congress Cataloging in Publication Data

Tuttle, W. C. (Wilbur C.), 1883–
    The tin god of Twisted River.

    (Atlantic large print)
    Originally published: London: W. Collins, 1942.
    1. Large type books. I. Title.
    [PS3539.U988T5 1984]    813'.52    83–15252
    ISBN 0–89340–714–3 (U.S. : lg. print)

British Library Cataloguing in Publication Data

Tuttle, W. C.
    The tin god of Twisted River.—
    Large print ed.—(Atlantic large print)
    I. Title
    813'.52[F]            PS3539.U988

    ISBN  0–85119–693–4

This Large Print edition is published by Chivers Press, England, and
John Curley & Associates, Inc, U.S.A. 1984

Published by arrangement with Singer Communications, Inc

U.K. Hardback ISBN  0  85119  693  4
U.S.A. Softback ISBN  0  89340  714  3

Copyright

# CONTENTS

# CHAPTER ONE

## COWBOYS IN TOWN

The little cow town of Calumet drowsed beneath a summer sun: a peaceful little village of false-fronted, unpainted frame buildings, many hitch-racks, sparsely populated with nodding saddle-horses, and little ambition to be anything but a cow town.

The streets were narrow, dusty, the sidewalks of warped boards clattered like unmusical xylophones beneath the tread of the booted cowboys, most of whom had draped themselves ungracefully in tilted chairs in front of the Ten Bar Saloon.

It was shady in front of the Ten Bar, and there was always a possibility of somebody's inviting them to have a drink. From the open door of the saloon came the cool odours of stale beer, the voices of a couple of seven-up players arguing over whether it was ethical or not for the man to turn three jacks in one game.

Two riders appeared at the north end of the street coming into town, their tired

1

horses poking through the dust, shuffling wearily. The leading rider was well over six feet tall, bronzed and gaunt, his wrinkled shirt-tail flapping in the vagrant breeze, attesting to the fact that he had been long in the saddle and had hunched his shoulders many times.

The face beneath his big sombrero was thin, bony, heavily lined. The nose was generous, the mouth wide, serious; the eyes set in a mass of grin wrinkles which belied the seriousness of the rest of his face.

The other cowboy was of medium build, bowlegged enough to fit a horse perfectly, and with a great breadth of shoulder. His face was as bronzed as that of his companion. Perhaps his features were a trifle more regular, just as serious, and his wide blue eyes with their innocent expression were out of accord with the rest of the man.

Their raiment was nondescript. The wind and dust of the dim trails had scoured and faded all the colour from their shirts, their bat-winged chaps were worn and wrinkled, and their sombreros were flopping and shapeless.

Their arrival caused the siesta-loving cowboys to lift their weary heads and give a little heed to the new arrivals. One of the cowboys tilted forward, the front legs of his chair clattering to the sidewalk.

'I'll be a derned liar if it ain't "Hashknife" Hartley and "Sleepy" Stevens!' he exclaimed. He got to his feet and leaned against a porch post.

'Yee-e-e-e-o-o-ow! Cowboys in town!' he yelped.

Hashknife Hartley's lips twisted in a wide smile, as he swung his horse up to a hitch-rack, threw one of his legs in a sweeping curve, almost hitting Sleepy Stevens, who had ridden in close beside him.

He whipped his tie-rope around the top pole of the rack, jerked the knot tight, yawned widely, and walked stiff-legged towards the Ten Bar saloon with Sleepy, the bowlegged one, following.

'Hyah, Hashknife,' greeted one of the cowboys, while the rest of them grinned widely and got to their feet.

'H'lo, Eddie, yuh old son-of-a-gun! How are yuh, Omaha? By golly, if there ain't ol' Pep'mint!'

They shook hands violently with Hashknife and fell upon Sleepy, *en masse*, while he blinked at them vacantly and begged Hashknife to introduce him.

'They're yore friends, Hashknife. Make me used to 'em.'

'Same old frozen-faced son of a gun, eh?' laughed one of the boys, slapping Sleepy on the back.

'Yore etiquette is plumb home-made,' said Sleepy indignantly. 'Oh, well, I'll shake hands with yuh, but you'll excuse me if I don't call yuh by name. He-e-ey! What do yuh think my hand is, anyway? Think it's a fringed decoration I'm wearin' on the end of my arm? Yo're goshawful vociferous for strangers.'

Sleepy flexed his fingers and glared at them. Slowly a smile spread across his face as he looked at each in turn.

'I've met you boys somewheres, ain't I?' he asked.

'We ain't never been nowhere,' denied Peppermint Poole.

'No'—Sleepy shook his head slowly— 'I'm wrong. Thought for a minute I knowed yuh, but yore faces looked kinda familiar. Lemme see.' Sleepy squinted thoughtfully for a moment. Then: 'Aw, I know now. I seen some pictures in a Sheep-Dip ad, and they looked so much like you gents—you'll pardon me, I'm sure.'

4

One of the cowboys made a dash at Sleepy, who eluded him and went into the saloon, followed by the rest of the crowd. Sleepy leaned on the far end of the bar while the rest of them stopped about midway.

'How long have you been away, Hashknife?' asked one of the boys, eyeing Sleepy, who was watching in the back-bar mirror for the first move.

'Six months,' Hashknife removed his sombrero and wiped his face. 'We left here early in March.'

'I thought yuh did. Old man Sibley has been askin' about yuh every time I seen him and wonderin' if yuh was comin' back.'

'What does he want?' asked Hashknife.

'I dunno, unless he's got some mail for yuh. Why don'tcha ask yore friend to have a drink with us, Hashknife?'

'He ain't no friend of mine.'

'Am I supposed to cry about it?' asked Sleepy seriously.

'He ain't in love, is he?' asked one of the cowboys.

'Most always,' grinned Hashknife. 'But this time he ain't. Sleepy thinks it's cute to act thataway. What's new in this country?'

'Nothin'. Thinkin' of stayin' awhile, Hashknife?'

'Not under the circumstances, Pep'mint. Well, here's swift death, gents.'

They drank deeply and clattered their glasses back on the bar, while Sleepy grabbed the bar bottle, lowered its contents an inch, and told the bartender to take it out of Hashknife's money.

Then he came up to the bar and shook hands seriously with each of the cowboys, telling each of them that he was glad to make their acquaintance. Amicable relations being restored, Hashknife decided to visit the postmaster and see if any mail was waiting for him.

Letters seldom reached Hashknife and Sleepy because they were continually on the move. Only in rare cases did they spend more than a month in any one place; usually less. Both of them were top-hand cowboys, capable of taking entire charge of any cattle outfit, their services always in demand. Yet they drifted hither and yon, seeking what they might find on the other side of the hill.

They would solemnly swear that they were looking for a peaceful range where they might settle down and live out the rest of their days; a range where all men were living at peace with other men; where honesty prevailed and where a quick draw was unknown.

But Fate and itching feet sent them into a land where there was little peace. Perhaps it was only the keen mind of Hashknife Hartley, the fighting ability of them both which brought peace to a troubled range.

They were fatalists, these two. To them all things were written in the Big Book, and they themselves only instruments of the moving finger that wrote their destiny.

'If there's pneumonia written after yore name, it's one cinch yuh won't never get killed with a bullet.'

Thus Hashknife, accompanied by a violent nod of agreement from Sleepy. The belief gave them confidence and the feeling that being in the right somehow gave them a decided advantage against a criminal.

Neither of them could split a second on the draw. There was nothing uncanny about their ability to draw a six-gun, nor were they of a deadshot variety. The West knew many gunmen who were swifter, more accurate than these two. Yet they lived unscathed. In sporting parlance it might be said that these men got the

7

'breaks' of the game, but were able to make the breaks for themselves.

They left the Ten Bar Saloon and crossed to the little post office, where they shook hands with the old postmaster.

'I 'lowed yuh'd come back,' he told them. 'I've got a letter fer you, Hashknife. Darned thing came in April. Didn't know where to catch yuh, so I kept it agin' the day you'd come back t' Calumet.'

'Must be pretty stale by this time,' smiled Hashknife as the old man handed him the letter.

He squinted at the postmark.

'Arapaho City, eh. Huh! Wonder who I know in Arapaho City?'

'Yuh might find out the answer inside,' murmured Sleepy. 'It prob'ly wasn't intended as a puzzle.'

Hashknife squinted sidewise at Sleepy, who registered innocence of any sarcasm. Hashknife drew out the letter and studied it closely. Several times he read it through before putting it back in the envelope.

'I reckon I better have a package of Durham, Mr. Sibley,' he said as he put the letter in his hip pocket and leaned on the counter where the postmaster kept his stock of candy.

'Yuh better mix me up two-bits' worth of candy while yo're at it. Them choc'lets look kinda faded, don't they?'

'Don't keep well in this climate, Hashknife. They're jist as good as ever, but they look weak. Eat 'em in the dark, and you'd never know they was mulatters.'

Hashknife paid for his tobacco and candy, and they wandered outside, where Hashknife reached into the bag, picked out a lopsided chocolate cream, and offered it to Sleepy.

'What was in that letter?' demanded Sleepy. 'Aw, to hell with that kind of candy!'

'That letter? Oh, yeah. Say, that was kinda queer. Read it.'

He handed the letter to Sleepy, sat down on the edge of the sidewalk and began making inroads on his bag of candy.

The letter was written on a piece of cheap tablet paper with a soft lead-pencil, undated, unsigned. It read:

Sir: We know you are coming to run the HL Ranch and you better not because you ain't needed here and your helth will be in dainger if you come here as we have got you spoted. Take warning by this and stay away

9

from around hear.

Sleepy folded up the letter and slid it into the envelope, after which he shoved the letter back in Hashknife's pocket and helped himself from Hashknife's bag of candy.

'Where's Arapaho City?' he asked indifferently.

Hashknife shook his head. His mouth was too full of candy just then. In a little while he wiped the back of his hand across his mouth and got to his feet.

'I was kinda candy-hungry,' he said slowly. 'But it don't take more'n a ton of that kinda stuff to cure me. What do yuh think of that billy-doo, Sleepy?'

'I dunno. Darned thing was written back in April. Mebby it was somebody's idea of a joke.'

'Mm-m-m-m. Let's go down and talk with the sheriff.'

'Well, all right. Whatcha goin' to do? Make a complaint?'

'He might know where Arapaho City is, Sleepy.'

'Oh, yeah. Well, I sure hope he don't. You ain't takin' that letter serious-like, are yuh, cowboy?'

10

'Not too serious, pardner. But it don't look like a joke. Who would take the trouble to warn me not to go to the HL Ranch when I never even heard of it? I'm just curious.'

'They tell about a cat that got curious.'

'Askin' won't get anybody killed.'

'Not if yuh stop at askin'. But I know you, dang yuh.'

Hashknife grinned thoughtfully as he headed for the sheriff's office. They knew Abe Gleason, the sheriff, and his greeting was not at all assumed.

'Come in, yuh darned pair of tumble-weeds!' he yelled, when the partners squinted in past the open door. 'By golly, I'm shore pleased to see yuh both. How are yuh?'

They shook hands joyfully and the big sheriff grinned from ear to ear.

'Long time we no see yuh, Abe,' said Hashknife, tilting a chair back against the wall. 'How's crime in this country?'

'Not a crime, Hashknife. We ain't had an arrest nor a complaint for six months. Tell me what you've been doin' since last March. By golly, yuh don't look like you'd lost many meals.'

'We've been eatin',' grinned Sleepy.

'Crime is kinda playin' out everywhere, Abe. Looks as if me and Hashknife will have to settle down at last.'

'It won't hurt yuh none. By golly, from what I can hear, you two jiggers has made life easy for a lot of sheriffs in six months. Now, what's on yore mind, Hashknife?'

Hashknife looked up from rolling a cigarette and squinted at the sheriff.

'Where's Arapaho City, Abe?'

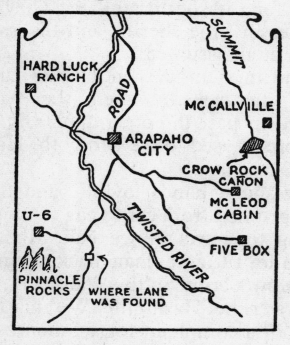

'Arapaho City? About ninety miles north-west of here. Up in the Twisted River country. Its plumb away from everybody and everythin', but she's one good cattle country, they tell me. I ain't never been up there, but that's where she is, Hashknife.'

'Twisted River country, eh? Have you got a brand register, Abe?'

The sheriff produced the required article, and it did not take Hashknife long to find that the HL outfit was owned by Henry Ludden. It was a combined initial brand, the right side of the H making the main stem of the L.

'Has there been any trouble up in that country?' asked Hashknife, placing the book on the sheriff's desk.

'Not that I know anythin' about, Hashknife. We're a long ways from Arapaho City. I don' even know the sheriff of that county, but I know his name—Pete Darcey. You aimin' to go up thataway?'

'If it's a good cattle country, Abe. Me and Sleepy are on the lookout for a ranch. We're tired of bein' what yuh call tumbleweeds.'

'Well, I suppose a feller does kinda want somethin' for himself after he gets old enough to have a little sense. But why don'tcha buy somethin' around here? We've got just as good range here as they have in Twisted River.'

13

'I reckon that's all true,' nodded Hashknife seriously. 'But I got a letter from a feller up in that country to-day and he kinda intimates that there's somethin' goin' on up there, and a feller kinda likes to get in on the ground floor, Abe.'

'Oh, sure. Didn't tell yuh what kind of a deal it was, did he?'

'No-o-o, he didn't, but he said he'd be expectin' me.'

Hashknife got to his feet and yawned widely.

'I reckon we'll stable our broncs, Sleepy, and get us each a good sleep. See yuh later, Abe. We won't leave until to-morrow.'

'By golly, you two are just like drops of quicksilver. Yuh won't stay put nowhere.'

'I know it, Abe. But we've got to go. This feller is waitin' for us.'

As they walked back towards the hitch-rack, Sleepy squinted at Hashknife and shook his head wearily.

'Goin' to get in on the ground floor, eh? More likely get six feet under the ground. Feller waitin' for yuh with a proposition. Don'tcha realize that letter was written in April, and this is the latter part of August?'

'That's all true, Sleepy. But some men do have the dangdest amount of patience.'

14

# CHAPTER TWO

## ARAPAHO CITY

It was four days after Hashknife and Sleepy had entered Calumet that Hank Ludden rode through the Twisted River hills astride a rangy grey horse. He might have posed for a painting of an old Indian scout as he rode along, carrying a Winchester rifle in the crook of his left arm, peering keenly from beneath the brim of his floppy sombrero.

Ludden was a big man, but stooped with age. His long grey locks straggled from under his hat and mingled with the heavy beard. His nose was slightly hooked and his keen eyes were almost hidden beneath jutting eyebrows, which were large enough to make a moustache for an ordinary man.

His arms were long and powerful and his gnarled, heavily-veined hands showed great strength. He rode easily in the saddle, guiding his grey horse in and out among the clumps of greasewood and sage without visible effort.

He rode down through a sandy, dry

15

water-course, disturbing the siesta of several head of cattle which had been drowsing in the shade of some cottonwoods, and drew up to squint at the brands.

After a few moments of inspection he rode on, heading for a rocky ridge which would give him a view of the surrounding country. The neutral colours of his faded clothes and the grey horse caused them to blend into the general scheme of the landscape, making them almost invisible at a short distance.

Ludden seemed to know where he was going. He rode almost to the top of the ridge, where he drew up and dismounted. The ride had evidently made him a trifle stiff, as he leaned his rifle against a rock and stretched his muscles.

He had dropped his reins, but now he studied the grey inquiringly.

'Goin' to stay there, Ghost? If I had a rope I'd tie yuh. Know danged well you'd bust a rein if I tied yuh with one. Oh, well, I reckon yuh won't go far.'

He picked up his rifle and went on up the slope, glancing back at the grey, which was standing still, its ears forward, watching its master. Ludden had never been quite successful in teaching Ghost to stand still with only the dropped reins.

Ludden angled along the ridge, being quite careful not to expose himself on the skyline, and came in behind a granite outcropping. He did not know that the horse was picking its way along behind him, stepping occasionally on the reins, but wise enough to lift its foot from the rein before going ahead.

The old man crawled slowly to the top of the granite pile, where he peered over the edge. Below him the hill sloped sharply, heavily covered with brush, down to an open swale or clearing which had once been the site of a ranch-house. One of the old buildings, or rather a part of it, was still standing at the far side of the clearing.

Almost in the centre of the clearing was a tumbledown pole corral, and it was on this corral that Ludden fixed his eyes. Inside the enclosure were several head of young stock milling around, looking for an exit, while just outside the corral gate were two men bending over a red yearling while a third man stood a little apart, holding a tight rope on the animal. A few feet away a tiny fire blazed, almost smokeless in the thin air.

17

Ludden's brows drew down over his eyes, and his gnarled fingers gripped the rifle tightly.

'Damn yuh, I knowed I'd find yuh if I kept at it!' he gritted to himself. 'It took me a long time and a lot of trips. I wish I could git down there among yuh.'

He scanned the hillside, looking for a possible chance to sneak up on them. They were at least two hundred yards away, and it was impossible for Ludden to identify them. Their horses were in the brush to the left of the corral, too well hidden for him to distinguish their colours.

He began to realize that the odds were in favour of the rustlers. Even if he did sneak in on them, three men are hard to handle. He knew they would kill him with no more compunction than they would show a rattlesnake.

He studied them closely, trying to note some action, some mannerism which might enable him to identify them. But he was looking down at them, almost a bird's-eye view, which made it more difficult for him.

One of the men walked over, placed some more wood on the fire, and appeared to be examining the branding-iron. Ludden scanned the surrounding country, looking for more stock.

'They're just startin',' he told himself. 'Iron ain't quite ready yet for the first one, and there's a dozen more in the corral. I'll take it easy, and mebby I can drop down close enough to identify some of 'em.'

He eased back slightly and reached towards his hip-pocket for his tobacco. Came the shrill nicker of a horse, and he whirled around to see Ghost standing full at the top of the ridge fifty feet away, reins dragging, as he bugled his call to the rustlers' horses.

'You damn' fool!' Ludden's angry snort was almost loud enough for the rustlers to hear.

They had heard the grey horse and could see against the skyline that it was carrying a saddle. Ludden turned and lifted his rifle. Two of the men had crawled swiftly through the corral fence darted among the frightened cattle, and were going out the other side before he could see just what had become of them.

The third one was running past the left side of the corral, going towards the horses, when Ludden fired.

The bullet struck just beyond the running man, and he jumped like a frightened rabbit.

As Ludden levered in another cartridge the two men sprang across the open space between corral and brush, leaving the old man swearing bitterly and searching the brush with eager eyes, his finger caressing the trigger of his thirty-thirty.

Ludden knew that they could not mount their horses without exposing themselves above the brushtop. So he crouched in the rocks, waiting for their next move. He felt sure that the three men were down there in the brush, waiting for him to expose his hiding-place.

He cursed the grey horse, which still posed on the ridge and waited patiently. Ten minutes passed without any sign of the rustlers.

Ludden squinted back at the grey and noticed that it was watching far to the left of where the horses had been. Suddenly the old man realized what had been done. Instead of mounting their horses, the rustlers had led them away, keeping to an old trail where the brush grew high enough to mask their passing.

He sprang to his feet and ran up the ridge, passing the grey, which snorted and moved aside. On up the rocky ridge ran the old man, almost out of breath, swearing at himself for letting them outwit him. About a hundred and fifty yards up the ridge beyond the horse he stopped and dropped to one knee.

Three riders were travelling away from him, going out of another swale. It was evident that these men had led their horses over into this swale, knowing that the point of the hill had cut off the view of the man who had shot at them, and were mounted and making their get-away complete.

It was a long shot. Carefully the old man twisted up the peep-sight, estimating rapidly.

'Five hundred yards,' he muttered. 'Rather be over than under. Movin' target at five hundred.'

He cuddled the butt of the rifle against his cheek, took a quick aim, and squeezed the trigger. The hills flung back the clattering echoes of the rifle shot, and the three riders flared out fanwise. It was evident that the bullet had struck close to them.

The rifle spoke again, and the left-hand rider was almost unseated when the bullet hummed off the ground under his horse's nose.

'Shootin' low,' muttered Ludden, adjusting his sight. 'Make it six hundred.'

The riders were spreading farther apart now, and almost to the skyline of the low saddle in the hills. Ludden sprawled on the ground, resting the rifle across a stunted greasewood. This time he was more careful. The rider was bearing to the left. The ivory bead completely covered horse and rider at that distance.

Then he swung the bead slightly to the left, squeezing the trigger as he swung the sight. Quickly he lifted his head and peered across the wide swale.

For a moment he thought he had nicked the man out of his saddle. The horse whirled and stopped, while the man recovered, straightened up in his saddle, and went on over the ridge. But he swayed in his saddle, humped over, until at that distance he looked like a pack on the horse instead of a human being.

'By God, I got one of 'em!' exclaimed Ludden. He rose to his feet and ran back to the grey horse, which snorted wildly but allowed the old man to catch him easily.

He mounted, and sent the grey down the hill on a stiff gallop. It was dangerously steep and brushy, but Hank Ludden cared nothing for this. He fixed his eyes on the low saddle in the hills where that humpbacked rider had disappeared, and let Ghost worry about the footing.

They crashed down through the heavy brush at the bottom, lurched over the bank of a washout, and headed for the top of the swale. Ghost was a willing runner, in spite of the fact that his rider was a heavy man.

Ludden kept a close watch on the skyline, thinking that the other two riders might ambush him at the crest of the hill, but there was no sign of them. He gained the top and drew rein, his eyes sweeping the hills ahead.

To the left and below him he could see part of the road which led towards Arapaho City. The grey was blowing heavily from the uphill run, and the old man eased himself in his saddle, wiping some blood off his face from the scratch of a greasewood limb.

Then he caught a glimpse of a rider going slowly towards the road. Ludden lifted his rifle, but lowered it again. He had no way of being sure that this was one of the rustlers, as the brush obstructed his view.

'I can see him plain when he reaches the road,' he told himself. 'Mebbe I better swing farther to the left.'

He turned his horse around, dropped below the skyline, and galloped to the left, intending to come back to the crest about two hundred yards farther along the hill.

\*　　\*　　\*

Hashknife and Sleepy had made no record time in covering the distance between Calumet and Arapaho City. It was a sparsely settled region they had traversed and the ranches were few and far between, but they carried enough food for their meagre wants.

'That feller has been waitin' since April,' said Hashknife, 'so a few extra days won't worry him none.'

And so they had dawdled through the hills, enjoying the sun, admiring the stars, until they struck a dusty road, winding in and out of the hills. And near where they struck the road they also found a weatherbeaten sign, pointing north:

## ARAPAHO CITY

And beneath the lettering some wag had written:

This is a quitclaim deed for my share of the darned thing.

Hashknife laughed softly as they rode on.

'Sounds interestin', Sleepy. That feller had a sense of humour and it was too much for him. Mebbe we'll ride past here, headed the other way, and leave two more quitclaim deeds for the next lucky men.'

'Be damn' lucky to ride past,' said Sleepy. 'I have a feelin' that Arapaho City is a buzz-saw village.'

'Yore liver's bad, Sleepy. This is a beautiful country. It ain't reasonable to suppose that a man could live amid such beauty and harbour mean thoughts. Chirk up, cowboy. Who knows what is ahead of us? Mebbe they'll send us to the legislature. Mebbe they'll—'

Hashknife drew up his horse, lifted himself in his stirrups, and scanned the hills. Sleepy drew rein and squinted at Hashknife.

'What's the matter?' he asked.

It came again—the faraway echo of a rifle shot.

'Nothin' but a rifle shot,' observed

25

Sleepy. 'If they're shootin' at us, they're sure doin' it at long range. Probably somebody fussin' with a coyote.'

As they moved forward again they heard the echo of another shot.

'Three times and out,' laughed Hashknife, scanning the hills. 'Anyway, it sounds like we were entering civilization.'

They rode along the crooked, dusty highway where the brush grew close to the wagon ruts, down through a wide swale, and into a straight stretch of road. About two hundred yards ahead they could see where the road turned abruptly to the right at the point of a hill.

To the left and ahead was the broken ridge with a low saddle, and farther to the left were high pinnacles like spires of a great cathedral.

Suddenly a rider broke through the brush about a hundred yards ahead. The road was not over twelve feet wide from brush to brush and the sun was almost directly in the eyes of the two cowboys.

It was like a short flash of a motion picture. The horse lurched across the road, the rider falling flat in the dust; nothing left except a little dust cloud, plumped up from the sprawling figure of the man, and the man himself, whose raiment blended well with the yellowish-grey dust. The dust cloud disappeared and there was nothing except the man, a hardly visible something, lying across the road. The horse had disappeared so quickly that neither of the cowboys could have sworn to its colour or size.

'Don't that beat hell?' queried Hashknife vacantly.

'Anyway,' said Sleepy dryly, 'it at least runs a dead-heat. Jist about what did happen, Hashknife?'

'I dunno. That danged sun was square in my eyes, but I think I seen a horse cross the road, drop its rider, and keep on goin'.'

'I'm glad that's what you seen, Hashknife, 'cause that was my impression. Mebbe we better look a little closer, eh?'

They spurred their horses forward, and were half-way to the prone figure when Hashknife's sombrero was almost jerked from his head. Came the sharp crack of smokeless powder from the crest of the ridge and the two cowpunchers instinctively whirled their horses to the right, crashing them straight through the brush.

Nor did they pause to investigate.

Sprawling low in their saddles, protecting their faces as best they might from the whipping branches, they rode at a headlong gallop, while bullets whispered around them as Hank Ludden frantically worked the lever of his rifle at the top of the ridge.

Luckily they struck down through a ravine before the old man could reload his rifle, and in a few minutes they were again on the road, but too far away for Ludden to see them.

'That's what I'd call a hell of a reception,' panted Sleepy as they drew rein and looked back, picking the pieces of broken limbs from their torn shirts. Sleepy had a long streamer of clematis vine around his neck, which made him look as if he had been roped. He threw it aside and squinted at Hashknife, who was examining the floppy brim of his sombrero, which had been torn by the bullet.

From off to their right came the *whang* of another shot, and they instinctively dodged.

'Aw, damn such a business!' snorted Sleepy disgustedly. 'Let's pull out, cowboy. C'mon.'

'Yuh don't have to coax me.' Hashknife rowelled his horse and they headed down the road at a stiff gallop.

They did not know that Hank Ludden was hot on their trail. He had shot at Hashknife from the back of the grey horse, which shifted slightly as he pulled the trigger, thereby causing him to miss by scant inches.

Hank had seen the rider fall from the horse and had decided that at least one of the rustlers was down and out. But he was not satisfied with one; so he swung his horse down the hill, angling over to the road, trying to get another shot at the two who had escaped him again.

The road entered Arapaho City from the south, but Hashknife and Sleepy did not enter boldly. An abandoned road which led past some old ranch buildings caught their fancy, and they circled the west side of the town, coming in at the north end, where they dismounted at a little-used hitch-rack.

Casually they walked to the corner and surveyed the main street of Arapaho City. Beside them was the Pekin Café, from which savoury odours assailed their nostrils. On the opposite side of the street was the Arapaho Livery and Feed Stable, in front of which was a huge water-trough, leaking badly and making a mud-hole in the street.

Farther up the street, on the same side, were the blacksmith shop, post office, and a number of saloons. On the opposite side were signs which proclaimed the Arapaho Hotel, Steve's Chop House, Arapaho Stage Office, Twisted River Mercantile Store, Deschamps Drug Co., Sheriff's Office.

The buildings and signs were weatherbeaten, grey with the street dust which billowed from the passing teams or riding horses. At the south end of the town was a blasted old cottonwood, like a great gnarled-hand, the forefinger pointing skywards.

A few wagon teams were tied at the hitch-rack, and a scattering of saddle-horses nodded in the sun. A couple of mongrel dogs, as if by mutual consent, met in the middle of the street, circled each other, growling deeply, turned, and went back to their respective shades as if the fighting game was hardly worth while under the circumstances.

Near the front of the Twisted River Mercantile Store a small boy laboured at the handle of a creaking old pump to which was attached a hose. The nozzle of the hose was held by a big man who industriously sprinkled the street adjacent to the front of the store, doing a thorough job in spite of the fact that the motive power's shirt had parted company with its pants and was in a fair way to complete exhaustion.

Hashknife and Sleepy grinned at each other and went into the Pekin Café, where a little old Chinaman grinned at them from the kitchen door, bobbing his head violently.

He came up and motioned them to a table, after which he began in a sing-song voice:

'Lo'sa beef, lo'sa po'k, veala stew, libba-bacon, ham a' egg—w'at yo' like, eh? Yo' like soup? Soup velley good t'day.'

'Ham and eggs,' said Hashknife, and Sleepy nodded to the Chinaman to bring him the same.

'Two ham a' egg, eh? Yo' want soup?'

'Is it compulsory?' asked Sleepy curiously.

'This time noodle.'

'No soup, Charley.' Sleepy grinned widely. 'Too hot.'

'Velly good.'

As the Chinaman bustled away a man came in, glanced sharply at Hashknife and Sleepy, and sat down near the door. He was a big man, slightly grey, with a heavily lined face and sad-looking eyes. He wore a faded blue shirt, overalls, and high-heeled boots. His belt sagged from the weight of his holstered gun, and the bottom of the holster was held down by a whang-leather string which circled the man's leg.

The Chinaman came bustling in, deposited knives and forks on the table, and hurried over to the newcomer, who lifted his head and smiled slowly.

'Hello, She'iff,' said the Chinaman. 'What y'like, eh? Got plenty good soup.'

'Ham and eggs, I reckon.'

'Yessah. Egg ve'y good to-day.'

He bustled away and Hashknife studied the profile of the big man—Pete Darcey, sheriff of Arapaho. As Hashknife studied the sheriff, he thought of the quit-claim notice on the old signboard: 'This is a quitclaim deed for my share of the darned thing.'

Perhaps the job of being sheriff of Arapaho had drawn the lines of sadness in this big man's face, thought Hashknife. The sheriff's hands were on the table—big, powerful hands, fit to grip the big gun which sagged at his hip.

The sheriff, after his first keen glance,

had paid no attention to Hashknife and Sleepy, but seemed to stare gloomily towards the sunbaked street.

Someone was coming down the board sidewalk, his boots rattling heavily on the loose boards. The sheriff shifted his gaze to Hank Ludden, who flung the door open and stepped inside the place. He was breathing heavily, carrying his hat in his hand.

'A kid at the pump told me you was here, Sheriff,' he said, leaning his hands on the sheriff's table as he recovered his breath. 'I was at yore office.' He looked back at the open door, took a deep breath, and turned to the sheriff.

'I connected with three rustlers at the old U6 Ranch. They had a dozen yearlin's in the corral and was warmin' their first iron. My horse nickered and ruined things for me. They fogged out, but'—Ludden paused for another deep breath—'I nailed one of 'em out in that low saddle east of the Pinnacle Rocks. He stuck to his horse until he hit the road and then he dropped.

'The other two tried to pick him up, but I drove 'em away, and I think they headed for town. I had a dead bead on one of 'em, but my horse moved and ruined it for me.'

The Sheriff got to his feet and headed for the door, followed by Hank Ludden, while Hashknife and Sleepy confined their attention to the Chinaman, who was bringing in their order.

The Chinaman glanced quickly at the backs of the two men who were going out.

'Bring us each half of the sheriff's order, Charley,' said Hashknife. 'He ain't got time to eat now, and we can sure eat an extra egg apiece.'

'Yessah, velly good. She'iff go way quick, eh?'

'Somethin' about cattle rustlers, Charley.'

'O-o-oh. Lustle cows, eh? Other man Hank Ludden, yo' *sabe?* Velly good man. I *sabe* him long time.'

'Cattleman?' asked Hashknife.

'Yessah. Plenty cow one time. Mebbe not so much now.'

'Uh-huh. Sell all his cows, eh?'

'No sell much. Plenty of cow get lost, yo' *sabe*. Long time cow get lost. No catchum lustler. Somebody name Hard Luck lanch. HL all same Hard Luck, yo' *sabe?* Hoo-o-o! Egg fry too damn' much!'

The Chinaman turned and galloped towards the kitchen, while Hashknife and

Sleepy squinted knowingly at each other and attacked their food.

'"Had a dead bead on one of 'em, but the horse moved and spoiled it,"' muttered Hashknife, quoting Hank Ludden's statement softly. 'I'll have to buy that horse a bale of hay as a reward. So that's the which of it, eh? By golly, we sure were lucky to save our scalps to-day, pardner.'

'And to-morrow is another day,' said Sleepy meaningly, as he tried to slide half an egg on to the blade of his knife.

'That sheriff looks sad enough to do anythin' and I don't want to run up against Hank Ludden, movin' horse or no movin' horse. This country sure looks salty to me.'

The Chinaman came shuffling back, bearing the sheriff's order, which he placed on their table.

'Is the sheriff a pretty good man, Charley?' asked Hashknife. He thought there might be a chance to get some information from the Chinaman, who seemed inclined to gossip.

'Yessah, velly good man. Be she'iff long time.'

'Uh-huh. Hank Ludden good man too, eh?'

'Yessah.'

'Good friend to sheriff?'

'Mebbe. I do' know. 'Lucky' Joe marry Ludden daughter.'

'Thasso? Who is Lucky Joe?'

'Dep'ty she'iff.'

'Been married long time, Charley?'

'Fo' five month. Ludden not like, I guess. Yo' want more coffee?'

'Yeah, I'll have some more,' said Sleepy. 'You make good coffee, Charley.'

'Yessah. My name Pat Lee.'

'Irish?' queried Hashknife seriously.

'Yessah, all same Irish.' He smiled blandly and headed for the kitchen.

'It's a great country,' declared Hashknife. 'They write a letter darin' yuh to come, shoot at yuh when yuh arrive, and name their Chinaman after an Irish saint.'

'If we had any sense, we'd pull out right away,' said Sleepy. 'The only thing we can gain here is a tombstone.'

Hashknife grinned softly and shook his head.

'That's for the Big Book to say, Sleepy. We don't keep our own books, so we don't know what our balance is. We've started in by eatin' the sheriff's meal. Who can say what will come next?'

# CHAPTER THREE

# A BUZZARD'S SHADOW

When Hank Ludden and the sheriff left the restaurant they went straight to the sheriff's office. The sheriff took a rifle from his gun-rack and led the way to the livery stable where he kept his horses.

'No use takin' anybody else, I reckon,' said the sheriff.

'Not much,' agreed Ludden. 'Who were the two strangers in Pat's place, Pete?'

'Never seen 'em before in my life,' replied the sheriff, lifting his saddle off a peg and throwing it on a roan horse which the stableman had led out to him. 'They were eatin' in there when I came in.'

He cinched his saddle and called to the stableman: 'Seen anythin' of Joe this mornin', Al?'

'Yeah. He said he was goin' out to the Five Box.'

'Thanks.'

Hank Ludden scowled at the mention of Joe Lane's name. He did not like Joe Lane, known as Lucky Joe, a rather handsome,

37

devil-may-care sort of person, deputy to Pete Darcey.

Hank Ludden's whole life had centred around his daughter Mary, and when Joe Lane came courting her, Hank lost no time in telling Joe that he was not eligible. Joe quietly informed Hank that he was not intending to marry him, and that his private opinions of his, Joe's, worth were merely one-man ideas.

Mary Ludden was a tall, slender, wistful-eyed girl with a wealth of chestnut hair, a pleasing personality, and a mind of her own. It is not at all unlikely that she could have had her pick of the young men of the Arapaho country, but she eloped with Lucky Joe Lane, and the world soured for Hank Ludden and 'Armadillo' Jones, his partner.

Mary and Joe took up their residence in Arapaho City, and Hank Ludden ignored their existence.

Every one in the country knew about it. Many of the old-timers shook their heads and said it was only another mark against the Hard Luck Ranch.

The first owner had been Jim Shafer, who registered the Circle S brand. He was an experienced cattleman from Texas.

Within a year he was thrown from a horse and instantly killed. His son, a wild-riding young man of twenty-five, took charge of the Circle S, carried on the business for a year, when he accidentally killed himself with a revolver.

Jim Shafer's widow sold the ranch to a Robert Morgan, who changed the brand to the Bar M and proceeded to get himself killed in a runaway in the yard of the ranch-house. Title descended to his brother, who operated the ranch-house successfully for over a year, only to be killed by a bolt of lightning on the ranch-house porch.

It was then that Hank Ludden and Armadillo Jones bought out the place, putting in every cent they had, changing the brand to the HL. But the proverbial hard luck of the ranch still remained. Try as they might they could not make it pay.

Instead of an increase there was a decrease. Each round-up showed them a loss of many head of stock, and in spite of continual vigilance their cattle vanished. The law had little appeal to either Hank or Armadillo. They had been partners for years—prospecting, mining, working with cattle.

The marriage of Hank Ludden had

broken their partnership, but the death of Mrs. Ludden, shortly after Mary was born, brought them together again stronger than ever. Armadillo even claimed a fifty-fifty interest in Mary, and he disliked Joe Lane as much as Hank Ludden did.

The sheriff and Hank Ludden rode out of Arapaho City together. There were many curious people who had seen Hank gallop into town, and they wondered what had happened to cause him to come for the sheriff, knowing that he had little use for any one connected with the office.

'You didn't look at this man, didja?' asked the sheriff as they galloped along the dusty road.

'Didn't take time. I seen him fall and he's there yet.'

The sheriff nodded grimly. The identity of this rustler might help to implicate the other two men. They swung around the right-hand turn at the point of the hill and came out on the straight piece of road. Hank Ludden raised in his stirrups and pointed up the road.

'There he is, Pete. Right where he fell.'

The dust-covered body was lying sprawled across the road just as it had fallen from the horse.

They reined their horses and dismounted. A soaring buzzard's shadow crossed the yellow dust between them and the body, and the sheriff glanced upwards, a scowl on his face. Then he strode forward, knelt in the dust, and turned the man over.

Hank Ludden cried out sharply and stepped back, while the sheriff looked up at him wonderingly.

It was Lucky Joe Lane, Ludden's son-in-law.

'Pete, it—it—' Ludden's hand shook as he removed his sombrero and wiped the cold perspiration from his brow.

'It can't be,' he whispered. 'Why, Joe Lane—'

'It's Joe Lane,' said the sheriff softly. 'My deputy, Hank.'

'Yeah, it's Joe Lane,' huskily. 'I—I don't quite *sabe* it, Pete.'

The sheriff squinted down at the dusty face of the dead man for a long time, while Hank Ludden gripped his cartridge belt and stared into space. He had killed the husband of Mary. For the first time in his life he realized that she loved this man— this dust-covered person who sprawled in the dust, his sightless eyes half-closed,

41

staring up at the blue sky. Hank remembered that Joe was so particular about his personal appearance, and it did not seem right for him to be sprawling in the dust. The sheriff looked up, and there was a suspicion of moisture about his eyes as he squinted at Hank Ludden and said:

'Hank, you ain't lyin' about this, are yuh?'

'Lyin' about what, Pete?'

'About findin' Joe with the rustlers. You ain't—'

The old man shook his head slowly.

'He was one of 'em, Pete. Good God, do yuh think, Pete, I didn't like Joe? Mebbe I was just selfish, I wouldn't murder a man. I—I didn't recognize him.'

The sheriff nodded slowly.

'I know how yuh feel, Hank. It hurts me a lot, I'll tell yuh. I liked Joe. Oh, why in hell do men do things like this, Hank? Joe didn't have to steal cattle. He could live on his salary. He could have every cent I own if he wanted it.'

'Mebbe I didn't treat him square,' whispered Hank. 'Mebbe he wanted to git even with me, Pete.'

The sheriff shook his head.

'No, Joe wasn't that kind of a person,

Hank. He's never said a word against yuh—not to me. Are yuh sure they was stealin' your cattle?'

'No. But they were stealin', Pete. Honest men don't corral yearlin' stock, build a brandin'-fire, and hightail it out of the country when a horse nickers.'

'No, they don't, Hank.' The sheriff grew thoughtful. 'Shall I tell Mary about it? She'll have to know about it, and you—'

'Go ahead and say it, Pete. I killed her husband.'

'I ain't blamin' yuh, Hank. It's hell, but directions says take it. I thought as much of Joe as I would of my own boy, but I'm not blamin' you. Things just worked out this way.'

'Others will blame me,' said Hank hoarsely. 'They know I didn't like Joe, and they'll say things.'

'Bein' human, they will,' nodded the sheriff. 'I wish we'd brought a wagon. Mebbe we can kinda drape him across my saddle, and I'll ride behind. I reckon that's the best thing to do, Hank.'

'Do yuh want me to go back with yuh, Pete?'

'Mebbe yuh better not, Hank. I'll fix things up as well as I can.'

43

'Thank yuh, Pete.' Hank Ludden held out his hand. 'So-long.'

Their hands met, gripped tightly, and the sheriff rode away, leaving Hank standing in the middle of the road looking after him.

The sheriff jogged around the curve and Hank went to his horse which he mounted and rode off the road to the left, heading towards the low saddle in the hills. The shock of finding he had killed Joe Lane took all the fight out of the old man, and all he could think of was how would Mary take the news.

He could mentally picture Pete Darcey telling her that Joe was dead and that her father had killed him. He wondered if there wasn't some way of telling her; some way of taking away the sting.

Could it have been an accident? he wondered. But he knew it was not. The three men were together, and it was merely a twist of fate which made Joe Lane the target instead of one of the others.

Ludden struck the trail where the rustlers had led their horses from near the corral, and came out into the clearing. The little branding-fire had long since burned itself out, and the corral was empty. Not a yearling remained within the enclosure.

'Came back and turned 'em all loose,' muttered Ludden. 'Not even ashes left of the brandin'-fire, and no brandin'-iron.'

He searched all around the place, but was unable to find any evidence that any misbranding had been attempted. Down in his heart he was glad that the sheriff had not come to the corral with him. It would have looked bad for him. Even the spot in the dust where the one animal had been thrown had been trampled by the feet of the escaping yearlings.

Ludden mounted his horse, climbed the ridge from which he had first seen the rustlers, and rode down across the hills towards the Hard Luck Ranch, northwest of Arapaho City.

It was not a pretentious place, this Hard Luck Ranch. The buildings had been placed on a sort of a low mesa, which jutted out into the wide mouth of a little valley like the prow of a battleship. A narrow, brush-lined stream wended its way around it.

Behind the small ranch-house the ground sloped sharply to the brush-covered hills. The ranch-house itself was originally a log building, but it had been added to until little of the original was left. The bunk-house was of logs, but the stables and sheds were of rough lumber, unpainted, scoured by age, the corrals of pole and lumber.

A huge live-oak tree shaded the front of the ranch-house, and at the rear grew a clump of big sycamores.

Roses climbed over the old porch, uncared for since Mary had left the ranch, and on the window-ledges were flowerpots containing what had once been geraniums, but were now mere wisps of dried substance, perished for want of moisture.

Armadillo Jones was sitting on his heels in the shade of the stable repairing a harness as Hank Ludden rode in past the corral and approached the stable.

Armadillo was a little man—thin, wiry, with a wrinkled parchment-like face and a bristling grey moustache. He was nearly bald, and when he lifted his eyebrows the wrinkles extended far above his original hair line.

Armadillo's nose was large, almost too large for his face, and his keen grey eyes were deeply set in a nest of hairlike wrinkles. His hands were long, bony, mahogany-tinted, and his legs, even in his squatting position, showed a decided tendency to bow.

One side of his face bulged from an enormous chew of tobacco which he shifted slowly; he spat deliberately and nodded to Hank Ludden, while his eyes squinted keenly at his partner.

Ludden dropped his reins and squatted beside Armadillo. It seemed the natural thing for him to do. Armadillo examined the mended strap, tested it by hooking one foot in a loop and pulling heavily. Then he tossed it aside, spat wearily, and leaned back against the stable wall.

'I found three rustlers at the old U6,' stated Ludden thickly. 'I dropped one of 'em in the road on the other side of Pinnacle Rocks.'

'Didja?' Armadillo spat viciously. 'Good! Who was he?'

'Joe Lane.'

'Oh, m' God! No!'

'Yeah.'

They didn't look at each other. Armadillo's jaws worked industriously and the long, lean fingers picked at the knees of his overalls, his eyes squinting painfully.

'Well,' he said slowly, 'I ain't a hell of a lot surprised. It'll be tough on Mary.'

'Yeah, it'll be tough on her, Armadillo.'

'Damn' tough!'

For several minutes neither of them spoke. Then Armadillo broke the silence.

'Speakin' of things bein' tough, Hank, I killed that old white leg'rn rooster for supper, but I'll be danged if I think we can eat him. I've had him on to b'ile for five whole hours now and about all he' done is to evaporate the water.'

'That's all right, Armadillo. I ain't got no appetite.'

'Appetite won't make no difference to that bird. The man that eats him has got to be plumb vicious.'

'I reckon we better go to town,' said Ludden wearily. 'Might as well face the music.'

'Yeah, we might as well.' Armadillo spat thoughtfully and got to his feet. 'I dunno what the music will be, though. It's gettin' to be a hell of a country when a feller has to get a rustler's name and address before shootin' him, for fear he might belong to a prominent family.'

'He was Mary's husband,' said Ludden softly.

'Good God, don't set there and tell me about it! Ain't I been thinkin' about it until m' ears ring? Do yuh think I'm so damn' ignorant that I don't realize a thing like that? Hank, I dunno'—Armadillo's voice softened—'It's terrible. I s'pose the best thing to do is to throw that rooster away and eat supper in Arapaho City.'

## CHAPTER FOUR

## SWAPPING LEAD

While the sheriff rode back to Arapaho City with the body of his deputy sheriff and Hank Ludden went back to the Hard Luck Ranch, trouble was brewing in another part of the Twisted River Range—Scotty McLeod's ranch.

It was a little ranch—just a two-room shack and a tumbledown stable—but within the fenced enclosure, bubbling from under a spreading sycamore, was a big spring from which flowed water that did not freeze, even in the coldest weather.

It was not hot water, but cool enough to drink at any time, yet it was practically the same temperature all the year around. And it was located on what the Five Box outfit claimed as their range. In other words,

Scotty McLeod was a nester, a fighting Scot who defied the Five Box to put him off his little ranch. 'Dutch' O'Day, owner of the Five Box, had tried in many ways to oust Scotty, but all his efforts had failed.

Not satisfied to hold the ranch and run his few head of stock, Scotty, angry at the Five Box, had secretly brought in a dozen sheep which he close-herded. To flaunt a dozen sheep in the face of the Five Box was like dangling a red rag in front of an angry bull.

Cowboys had taken long shots at the sheep in Scotty's front yard, but without any casualties. Perhaps it was because they feared Scotty's skill with a rifle that they did not come close enough for a good shot at the sheep.

But on this day Scotty had been to town, and in the meantime his sheep had managed to get out of the yard. Scotty noticed that about half of them had vanished when he returned; so he intended to fix the fence before cooking himself a meal, resolving to round up the lost sheep right away.

He was absorbed in the latest newspaper while his coffee-pot boiled over when he heard a noise at the door. Looking up, he beheld the face of Ben Corliss, foreman of the Five Box, a big, lean-faced man with a broken nose. Corliss carried a six-shooter in his right hand with which he motioned to Scotty.

Corliss was a much bigger man than Scotty, who was what might be termed undersized. Scotty's hair was a flaming red, and the colour of his chin was almost the same tint, which exaggerated the blue of his eyes.

'What do ye want?' asked Scotty coldly.

'C'mere, nester.' Corliss motioned him outside. 'Don't make no fool break for a gun, McLeod.'

'I'm no fool!' snapped Scotty.

He followed Corliss out in the yard, where he beheld his best sheep, now nothing more than an inanimate drag on the end of Corliss's lariat rope.

'There's four more back in the hills—dead,' said Corliss. 'If you think you can turn sheep loose in these hills, you've got another think comin'.'

'They got away,' said Scotty simply. 'I was in town.'

'Got away, eh?' Corliss backed to the carcass of the sheep and removed his rope, which he coiled and threw over the horn of

51

his saddle.

'You better imitate the sheep, McLeod. We've tolerated you about as long as we care to. *Sabe?* We need a reason to wipe you out, and yore sheep furnished it. Now, you high-tail it out of there before we come back.'

'Ye mean to come back, do ye?' Scotty smiled softly. 'Well, I'll try to meet ye with a gr-r-rin, Cor-r-r-lis.' Scotty began burring his *r's*, which indicated that he was getting angry.

'Yeah, we'll be back,' snarled Corliss.

'I'll tr-ry to be here.'

'Yuh will, eh? Fine. Walk down to the gate with me, McLeod. I'm not goin' to take any chances on you pottin' me with yore rifle from the house.'

He forced Scotty to go with him to the gate and stand there while he mounted his horse.

'Now you just try runnin' back to the house,' laughed Corliss. 'The rest of my outfit are settin' out there in range of here, and they'll make a sieve of yore shack in about a minute. So go slow, you sheep-lovin' pup.'

Corliss touched the spurs to his horse and galloped away, while the little Scot

52

ducked low and ran swiftly towards his doorway, zigzagging his course. A moment later he knew that Corliss had not lied.

A bullet struck in the gravel just beyond him, throwing up a little spurt of dust and hitting the house a resounding *thwack*! Another struck near his feet, ricochetted and broke one of the shack windows.

But before another one could throw gravel in his face, he dived through the doorway, rolled across the floor, and lifted his rifle from where it stood in a corner of the room.

Then he ran back, wriggled out through an open window and ran to the corner, where a scraggly bush gave him a little cover, and just beyond him he could see two horses. A man got into a saddle and seemed to be waving an arm at Corliss.

But Corliss was riding into heavier brush now, and Scotty could not see him plainly. The other man had shifted his position, which rather confused Scotty, but as he squinted at the brushy hillside he could see a moving horse. He was not exactly sure as to the identity of the rider, nor whether there was a rider, but decided that at least he would make somebody move quickly.

Scotty did not look any farther. He lifted

his forty-five-seventy rifle, swung the muzzle against the corner of the house, caught a quick sight, and squeezed the trigger.

The big rifle jerked violently and its crashing report was flung back by the hills, while a cloud of smoke drifted back into Scotty's face.

He lowered the muzzle quickly. He could see a saddle-horse, but there was no sign of the rider. The horse turned and ran over the brow of the hill. Farther to the left someone was shooting at the house, and Scotty could hear the bullets hitting the walls. He levered in another cartridge and waited for someone to expose himself.

*     *     *

The entrance of the sheriff with his dead deputy caused Arapaho City to wake up. Joe Lane had been a favourite in the town, and his demise was more or less of a shock to every one. The sheriff went straight to his office, where several men helped him place the body on a cot. To all their questioning the sheriff turned a deaf ear until the coroner had been notified. Then he gave them this short statement:

'Hank Ludden caught him rustlin' cattle and shot him. Hank didn't know who he was. There was two other men with him and they were operatin' at the old U6 corral.'

Hashknife and Sleepy were in the crowd which grouped around the doorway of the sheriff's office, and it seemed to Hashknife that no one believed the sheriff.

'Rustlin', hell!' snorted a cattleman. 'Good excuse.'

The sheriff looked sharply at the speaker, but did not reply. He had expected just such a sentiment.

'Speakin' of shootin',' remarked a fat-faced cowboy, whose legs were too short for his barrel-like body, 'I jist rode in from the Five Box, and I shore hears a hell of a lot of shootin' goin' on over towards that nester's place. Sounded like Fo'th of July.'

'Prob'ly somebody takin' pot-shots at the damn' shepherd,' laughed another. 'I hear he's got twelve sheep. He's sure due to grab a harp pretty soon.'

The coroner arrived, and the sheriff ushered him in, shutting the door against the rest of the crowd which resented such practice and repaired to the nearest saloon to talk things over.

Hashknife and Sleepy lingered until the sheriff came out, which was about a minute after the rest of the crowd had vanished. He squinted at them, stopped as if waiting for them to ask a question, and then walked to his horse.

'You goin' over to the nester's place?' asked Hashknife.

The sheriff paused and looked at them. It was rather unusual for a stranger to interest himself in this way.

'Why?' he asked shortly.

'Thought we might ride along and talk with yuh.'

'Well—' The sheriff paused. 'Talk about what?'

'Oh cabbages and kings, mebbe.'

'Cabbages? What's the joke, stranger?'

'No joke. Wait until we get our horses and we'll ride out there with yuh. It might interest yuh to know that we was the two men that Hank Ludden missed, when his horse moved.'

'Ye-e-eah?' The sheriff's mouth opened widely, and his right hand slipped from his hip, where it had been resting.

'He mistook us for the two rustlers,' explained Hashknife quickly.

The sheriff's mouth resumed its normal

expression and he nodded slowly.

'Go get yore horses,' he said.

And then he added as an afterthought when he realized their horses were tied:

'Swing around the town and meet me outside, will yuh?'

They mounted and left Arapaho over the same route they had used in entering. A quarter of a mile from town they overtook the sheriff, who spurred his horse to a gallop.

'We'll talk later!' he yelled at them. 'Prob'ly have more time later on.'

That arrangement was all right with Hashknife and Sleepy. They realized that here was a sheriff who knew the value of swift action, and they appreciated the fact that he could wait to hear what they had to say.

About a mile from town the road to the nester's ranch turned sharply to the left, while the main road continued to the Five Box. There was no let-up in speed. The sheriff sat his horse well, scanning the country as he rode.

Suddenly he jerked his horse sharply, almost blocking the two men behind him.

'Didja hear that shot?' he asked.

It came again, the echoing bang of a rifle,

and not so far away.

'C'mon!' The sheriff rowelled his horse and they went pounding up the old road, heading for the sound of the guns.

'Mebbe some fool is target-shootin'!' yelled the sheriff, 'but we've got to find out.'

The road led down through a ravine, twisting in and out of the brush, came out into a little valley, studded here and there with oak clumps, sloping gently upward towards where the nester's cabin was located.

The three riders drew rein and scanned the surrounding hills. To the right of them and up on the side of the steep hill a huge out-cropping of granite jutted out. And, as they scanned the hills, from behind this granite dike came the *whang* of a high-powered rifle.

The three men instinctively ducked their heads. Hashknife and Sleepy grinned foolishly at each other, while the sheriff whirled his horse and rode closer to the foot of the hill.

'Hey!' he yelled. 'What in hell do yuh think yo're doin' up there?'

From among the rocks lifted the head and shoulders of a man. He peered down at them, wondering, no doubt, what it was all about.

'*Spow-ee-e-e-e-e!*'

A bullet ricochetted off the rock beside him, and he ducked like a rabbit, while from farther up the valley came the roar of a black-powder rifle cartridge.

'What's goin' on around here?' yelled the sheriff.

'Go up and muzzle that damn' nester!' yelled the man behind the rock. 'You dang near got me killed. Who in blazes are you, anyway?'

'I'm the sheriff!'

'Oh, that's different. This is Corliss, Pete. Go up and stop that damn' nester, will yuh? He's killed Oscar Naylor, and he's got Moon down in a coyote hole across the canyon.'

'Yuh say he's killed Naylor?'

'An hour ago, yeah. Look out for him, Pete. That damn' fool can hit yore belt-buckle at half a mile.'

No doubt this was a gross exaggeration of Scotty's marksmanship, but showed what Ben Corliss thought of it after an hour of swapping lead with him.

The sheriff drew out a none-too-clean white handkerchief, grasped it by one corner, and turned to Hashknife.

'You better stay here, gents. This nester might 'a' gone crazy or colour-blind, and he sure can shoot.'

'Better all three go,' said Hashknife. 'Take it slow, I'd say. Show him we ain't tryin' to rush him.'

'Good idea. C'mon.'

They went slowly up the road and soon came in sight of the little shack. The sheriff held up his flag of truce, waving it gently, while Hasknife and Sleepy rode one on each side of him, expecting any moment to have the nester fire upon them.

But nothing happened, and they dismounted at the gate. Several dead sheep were scattered around the yard, attesting to the fact that all the shots had not been fired at Scotty. Both front windows had been shot out.

'Hey! McLeod!' yelled the sheriff.

'And what would ye be wantin', wavin' your white rag and comin' slow?'

Scotty had stepped out from the rear of the house and was looking them over.

'Oh, it's the sher-r-riff, eh?'

'Yeah,' nodded the sheriff, walking towards Scotty.

'Did ye silence thim br-r-rave

cowpunchers?' he asked, waving one hand in the general direction of his enemies.

'They're all through, McLeod. What started all this?'

Scotty rubbed his nose thoughtfully.

'Me sheep, Sheriff. Several of thim got away, and the Five Box outfit killed 'em. Ben Corliss came with one of 'em on a r-r-rope, and he warned me to leave. He forced me to accompany him to the gate, and when I started back his cohorts star-r-rted shootin' at me. I got in the house, took me gun, and returned their fire. We've been at it over an hour now, so I guess there's been no harm done.'

'Corliss says you killed Oscar Naylor.'

'I don't know about that. We had it hot and heavy for a while. They've killed all me sheep, I think, and my house will leak like a sieve in the next rain.'

'Give me your gun, McLeod,' ordered the sheriff.

The Scot frowned slightly, but grinned as he handed the gun across.

'I'd as soon, Sheriff. I shot me last cartridge a while ago.'

He glanced towards the gate and his face hardened. Corliss was walking towards him, rifle in hand.

'You dir-r-rty pup!' gritted Scotty.

Corliss paid no attention to him, but spoke directly to the sheriff.

'Moon just yelled that he had found Naylor, and he's dead.'

The sheriff sighed deeply and looked at Corliss.

'What's yore side of this, Ben?'

'Go ahead and lie,' said McLeod.

Corliss scowled and started towards Scotty, but the sheriff stepped between them and held out his hand to Corliss.

'Give me yore gun, Ben. Yo're six-gun too.'

Corliss handed over the two weapons, looking sharply at Hashknife and Sleepy, two men he had never seen before. The sheriff knew that Corliss was wondering who they were, but he was in no position to say.

'The nester's sheep got loose,' explained Corliss. 'You know how we feel about sheep, Pete. We stopped some of 'em and I roped one, which I brought down here with me. I told McLeod what I thought of a sheep-raising nester, and told him he better call it a day and pull out of here.

'I made him walk to the gate with me because I didn't want him too close to his rifle when I was ridin' away. As soon as I pulled out he ran into the house and started shootin' at us. Naylor and Moon were up there on the hill, and he got Naylor the first shot. Anyway, Moon says he got him with the first shot.

'Naylor didn't know that McLeod had run back for his gun, so he didn't have a chance in the world. I wasn't back to 'em when the shootin' started, and he drove me off that side of the valley. That's how I happened to be up there behind that granite cliff where yuh found me.'

The sheriff turned to McLeod.

'How about it, McLeod?'

'Par-r-rt true, par-r-rt lies, Sheriff. They were shootin' at me before I got back to the house. I was lucky to get in there alive. If Naylor didn't know the shootin' had started he must have been deaf, because there were several shots fired before I got me gun, and there was more fired before I had any chance to take par-r-rt.'

'Yo're a liar!' snapped Corliss.

'Drop that, Ben,' warned the sheriff. 'This is no place to discuss it—not between you and McLeod.' He turned to McLeod. 'I'm sorry, but I'll have to arrest you, McLeod. I'm not saying' that you were not justified in what you have done, but a man has been killed, and that demands an investigation.'

'I suppose so,' nodded McLeod. 'I'm not sorry, Sheriff. They forced me to it, and if I killed a man, he had his chance the same as the rest of us. It was war-r-r, and no favours. Perhaps I'm sorry it was Naylor instead of Corliss, because I had no quarrel with Naylor.'

'You'll hang just as high for Naylor as for me,' said Corliss angrily.

'But with less satisfaction,' replied Scotty coldly.

The sheriff turned to Corliss. 'You go back and help Moon bring Naylor's body down to the road. We'll saddle McLeod's horse and meet you there.'

'All right, Sheriff.'

Corliss turned and hurried back, while the four men went to McLeod's little stable and let him saddle his own horse. Scotty did not complain until the sheriff assured him that he would get a fair trial.

'Will I?' he asked coldly. 'With a cattlemen's jury?'

'The sheep were against yuh, pardner,' said Hashknife kindly. 'That was your mistake.'

64

'I'll admit it,' said Scotty. 'I'm bullheaded. Since I've been here I've fought to live. The Five Box is a big outfit for one nester to fight. I was whipped a long time ago, but I didn't know it.

'I was a fool to bring the sheep. It was like takin' a big roll of bills from your pocket, placin' thim on the table behind your poker chips, tryin' to frighten a gambler. I wanted to make the Five Box fightin' mad'—Scotty laughed bitterly—'I think I made a big success of it, too.'

'And the witnesses are two to one,' reminded Hashknife.

'Aye, that's true. But so was the shootin'.'

'And yuh never can tell,' agreed Hashknife, smiling at Scotty's optimism.

They led Scotty's horse back to the other horses, where they all mounted and rode back down the little valley. Down near the spot where they had discovered Corliss, they found him and Moon with the body of Oscar Naylor. Moon was a short, heavy-set cowboy, with a round face and an upturned brown moustache.

# CHAPTER FIVE

# A MAN IN JAIL

There was a certain resemblance between the face of Jim Moon, nicknamed 'Honey,' and that of the usual artist's conception of the Man in the Moon. But Honey Moon was neither smiling nor beaming. He scowled heavily at Scotty McLeod and waited for the sheriff to speak.

The sheriff's examination of Naylor was brief.

'Dead enough,' he said coldly. 'Rope him to his saddle and we'll go to town.'

'Ain't yuh goin' to arrest that damn' nester?' asked Honey Moon.

His voice was husky, high-pitched.

'Tub o' lar-r-rd!' snorted Scotty.

'The nester is under arrest,' said the sheriff. 'If you've got any remarks to make to my prisoner or about him, don't let me hear 'em. I've taken charge of him, Honey, and it's up to me to protect him. *Sabe?*'

'Oh, all right,' grudgingly.

Hashknife liked Pete Darcey for that remark. It showed that the sheriff was playing square with his prisoner.

'And I want you boys to pack a message to Dutch O'Day,' said the sheriff as they roped Naylor's body to his horse. 'You tell O'Day that I'm holdin' him responsible for anythin' that might happen to McLeod's few head of stock or to his little ranch while McLeod is in my charge.'

'You don't think O'Day would bother his damn' stuff, do yuh?' asked Corliss indignantly.

'No matter what I think, Corliss. You take the message.'

'Oh, I'll tell him, all right. But Dutch O'Day ain't a man who—'

'I'm not askin' for any pedigree, Corliss. I know O'Day as well as you do. I'm not makin' him responsible for only his own acts. I'm includin' the Five Box outfit.'

'Oh, all right. Do yuh want me and Honey to go to town with yuh, Pete?'

'Not unless you want to.'

'We better go,' advised Honey Moon. 'Naylor was my bunkie, and I want to see that nester behind the bars.'

The sheriff tied off his lash-rope, picked up the lead rope on Naylor's horse, and mounted his own animal. Corliss had been rolling a cigarette, his eyes squinting

67

inquiringly at Hashknife and Sleepy.

'Pete, who are these two men?' he asked abruptly.

The sheriff looked at Hashknife and Sleepy, frowned slightly, and rubbed the back of his hand across his chin. He knew no more about them than Corliss did.

Hashknife grinned slowly and shifted in his saddle.

'We're the Smith brothers,' he said easily. 'I'm the tallest, and he's'—pointing at Sleepy—'the shortest.'

Hashknife said it so earnestly that every one took it for granted until Scotty McLeod's sense of humour caused him to snort audibly. The sheriff turned his head and looked at his prisoner reprovingly.

'Friends of the nester, eh?' growled Corliss, who had misconstrued Scotty's snort.

'Yuh never can tell,' said Hashknife seriously.

'Well, we better be movin' along,' said the sheriff, and the cavalcade headed for Arapaho City.

Several times during the trip Hashknife caught Scotty McLeod looking at him with a grin on his lips. Scotty was evidently still amused at Hashknife's self-introduction.

When almost to town Hashknife spurred in close to the sheriff and told him of seeing Joe Lane fall from his horse and of their narrow escape from Hank Ludden's bullet. The sheriff listened closely, but made no comment.

'Do you know anybody around here?' he asked.

'Not a soul, Sheriff.'

'Lookin' for work?'

'Nope. We might take jobs, but we're never lookin' for work.'

The sheriff grinned and shook his head.

'I dunno what you'll be able to find around here, Smith. You sure showed up on a lively day. This is the most killin' we've ever had in one day. I know I've got to appoint me another deputy, dang the luck.'

They rode in to the main street of Arapaho City and to the front of the sheriff's office. The word spread quickly, and they had hardly dismounted when men came running from all directions to stare at the cavalcade and ask questions.

They crowded around the body of Naylor, questioning the two cowboys from the Five Box, while the sheriff took Scotty McLeod through his office and locked him in a cell at the rear.

But the crowd could get no satisfaction from questioning Corliss and Moon, so they surrounded the sheriff when he came out.

'Back up, you fellers!' snapped the sheriff. 'Some of the Five Box outfit got smart with McLeod, tha's all. Give me room to unleash that body, will yuh?'

'The nester killed Naylor?' asked one of them.

The sheriff did not reply but busied himself with the ropes.

'Here comes Mrs. Lane,' said one of the crowd, as if warning them. The talking ceased and several men stepped off the sidewalk, glancing quickly at the tall, slender girl who was hurrying towards them. She was wearing a kitchen apron over her white dress and there was a smudge of flour across her nose and cheek.

She stopped short when the crowd moved aside and she could see the body roped to the saddle. The sheriff turned and looked at her, but his glance strayed quickly away and around the crowd as if looking for someone to help him handle the situation.

The woman came closer, her eyes wide

70

with apprehension. She stumbled over a warped board, stopped. A breeze blew a lock of hair across her eyes and she brushed it back with a trembling hand. A man swore softly and moved away, going slowly across the street. Two more followed his example, glad to get away.

'Pete, what—is—it?' Mrs. Lane spoke haltingly.

The sheriff looked at her. His lips twisted painfully.

'This is—is Naylor,' he said. 'You knew Naylor, Mary.'

'Yes, I—I knew him.' Her voice was strained hoarse with emotion as she came slowly forward to the edge of the sidewalk.

'I—I knew Naylor. You say that is Naylor? Somebody'—she tried to smile, choked—'somebody said it—it was Joe. But it wasn't Joe. It was Naylor. Oh, I'm sorry it—it had to be anybody.'

'Yes'm.' The sheriff looked appealingly around. This was making it worse. Someone had told her that Joe was dead, and now the shock would be just double. She was trying to smile, and he was going to tell her the truth. He moved towards her, came to the edge of the sidewalk, his hands clenched tightly.

71

'Mary,' he whispered, 'I've got to tell yuh the truth. I was intendin' to come right to yuh, right after it happened, but the other deal came up and I didn't have time. Joe got—'

The sheriff stopped and turned away. He could not bear to look at the expression of her face. She knew now. The smudge of white flour was not visible now. Her lips were compressed tightly and her eyes were staring vacantly into space.

Hashknife stepped to the sidewalk beside her. He expected her to faint. She interpreted his move and looked up at him.

'Thank you,' she whispered bravely. 'I'm all right.'

'You've got nerve,' said Hashknife softly. 'Keep hangin' on to it, ma'am.'

'Where is Joe?' She turned to the sheriff, who was mopping his brow with a gaudy-coloured handkerchief.

'They moved him down to the doctor's home,' offered one of the men.

'Mary, you hadn't better go down there,' advised the sheriff. 'You wait until yuh kinda get over the shock.'

'Get over the shock?' Her lips trembled and she choked back a sob. 'How did it happen? Who did it?'

'Good God!' muttered one of the men hollowly.

And while the woman waited for someone to tell her, the crowd drifted across the street, singly and in groups, leaving only the sheriff, Hashknife, and Sleepy to tell her. It was too much for the sheriff, who turned to Hashknife.

'Yo're a stranger here, Smith. For God's sake, take her away from here and tell her about it. If you'll do this for me, I'll never forget it.'

'But—but what is it all about?' asked Mary Lane blankly.

Hashknife touched her on the arm.

'If yuh want to walk down to the doctor's office, I'll go with yuh, ma'am. Mebby it'll be easier for me to tell yuh all about it.'

Without any comment she walked with him, while the sheriff and Sleepy looked after them, thankful that Hashknife was game enough to accept the delicate task of explaining things to her.

'I think it was an accident.' Hashknife could think of no better way to break the news to her.

'You mean, he was accidentally—'

'Yes'm. Anyway, it looks thataway to me. Yore father was lookin' for rustlers,

73

they tell me, and he runs into three of 'em. Somehow they got away from him, and after—'

'My God!' Mary stopped and stared at Hashknife. 'You mean that my father shot Joe?'

'Well, I tell yuh I think it was an accident. Yore dad seen this man ridin' along and he—'

But there was no use in going further, and he knew it.

'That's why they wouldn't tell me,' she said painfully. 'All those men walked away, looking so queerly at me. My own father shot Joe. He thought Joe was a rustler and they—'

She shuddered, and Hashknife grasped her arm.

'No, I'm not going to faint,' she told him. 'You are a stranger and you don't know about things. They all know that my father disliked Joe. They'll say that he killed him out of spite.'

'I don't think your father would murder a man.'

Mary Lane looked at Hashknife, her eyes filled with horror and pain, but her lips were firm now.

'No, he wouldn't murder,' she said

74

slowly. 'He thought Joe was a rustler and Joe can't prove that he wasn't.'

Hashknife shook his head. Two men were crossing the street from a hitch-rack, and Hashknife recognized one of them as Hank Ludden. The other was Armadillo Jones. Mary Lane saw them, and turned her head away.

They came to the edge of the sidewalk and stood together looking at Mary. Armadillo squinted at Hashknife, and there were tears in his eyes, or it might have been caused by the sun and the dust.

Mary looked up at Hashknife and said: 'I will go the rest of the way alone. Thank you for telling me, Mr. Smith.'

She turned and walked away, not even looking at the two men. They followed her with their eyes until she turned the corner, going past the old, blasted cottonwood which pointed a crooked forefinger skyward as if promising a retribution.

'You shore raised hell,' declared Armadillo slowly and distinctly. 'Never even looked at us.'

'Can yuh blame her?' asked Ludden hoarsely.

'Well, my God, I never shot any of her relations!' retorted Armadillo hotly. 'Jist because we're pardners it ain't my fault if yuh shoot somebody.'

Hank Ludden turned and walked slowly back towards the hitch-rack. Armadillo squinted at Hashknife and turned his head to watch Hank cross the street. After a moment he hitched up his belt, spat reflectively, and followed Hank.

Hashknife went back to the sheriff's office. They had placed the body of Naylor on a cot. The bullet had torn its way through the man's body, making a wicked wound, but the sheriff was unable to say whether the man had died instantly or not.

'I seen Naylor fall,' said Moon, who had come back to the office after Hashknife and Mrs. Lane had walked away.

'I wasn't far from him. We seen Corliss comin' back, so we swung around, intendin' to ride over the ridge, when all at once I hears the bullet hit Naylor.

'He didn't say anythin'—jist fell off. I swung my horse around to go back to him, but that damn' nester started heavin' bullets so close to me that I unloaded off my bronc and dug myself in. My gosh, that jigger sure can shoot straight.'

Hashknife and Sleepy went outside, and in a few minutes the sheriff joined them.

'Goin' to eat somethin',' he told them. 'C'mon and have a bite with me. Have a cup of coffee or anythin'. I want to hear how Mary Lane took the news.'

\* \* \*

They walked down to the Pekin Café, where the Chinaman with the Irish name grinned at them and hastened to take their orders.

'I told the lady all about it,' said Hashknife. 'Yuh can imagine how she'd take it, can't yuh? But she didn't scream nor faint, if that's what yuh mean.'

'She's got nerve,' mused the sheriff. 'Mary loved Joe Lane. I ain't never been married, but if I ever do, I hope my wife will like me as well as Mary liked Joe.'

The sheriff sighed deeply and drummed on the table with his big fingers.

'This has been a hard day for Arapaho City. Two dead men, a broken heart, and a man in jail.'

'What will they do to the nester?' queried Sleepy.

'I dunno.' The sheriff squinted gloomily at the wall. 'The sheep will hurt his chances with a jury.'

77

'Only twelve sheep,' said Hashknife.

'Numbers won't matter, Smith. Sheep are hated in this country. If one of the Five Box had killed McLeod, it wouldn't be worth my while to arrest them, because any jury in this county would turn 'em loose.

'I had to arrest McLeod. Perhaps he wasn't to blame. I know those Five Box boys, and they're wild as hell. But I had to do it, as much to save him as anythin'. They'd go back and kill him sure. This way there's a chance for him to get off with manslaughter.'

'Yuh spoke about Dutch O'Day,' reminded Hashknife.

'Yeah. Dutch owns the Five Box outfit. He's a wizened little old Irishman, with a temper of the devil. Several years ago he got both legs broke in a runaway. Wheels went over both legs below the knee.

'The bones were crunched pretty bad, I reckon. Anyway, they didn't knit well. The doctor managed to save his legs, but little good it did him. He'll never walk. All day long he sits on the porch of the Five Box ranch-house and curses everything and everybody. Got a big Chink cook who carries Dutch where he wants to go, and takes care of him. Dutch curses Long How, calls him How Long, but the Chink just grins.

'Once in a great while Dutch comes to town. It ain't often. He thinks everybody is laughin' at him, but they're not, of course. Who would laugh at a cripple? His mind must be twisted a little over his trouble. He probably egged the boys into makin' an attack on McLeod. Dutch has tried to force McLeod off that place, but didn't quite make it. Dutch wants that spring for a winter waterhole.'

'Why didn't he buy McLeod out?' asked Hashknife. 'It would be worth it to the Five Box, I think.'

'Buy, hell! Do you think Dutch O'Day would buy from a nester? Not that it wouldn't be the square thing to do, Smith, but the principle of the thing would be all wrong. If McLeod goes to the penitentiary, the Five Box will take back that spring, but I think O'Day is wise enough to order hands off until the case is settled.'

'How many punchers does O'Day usually have?'

'Four. Oh, sometimes he puts on extra men. Corliss, Moon, Naylor, and Dayne have been with him a long time. I dunno who he'll get to take Naylor's place.'

'What kind of a feller is this Corliss?'

'All right. He's the foreman. You've got to credit him with havin' patience. Anybody that'll take orders from O'Day must have patience. He has to handle most of O'Day's business because O'Day can't get around. Corliss is all right. He's a darned good cowman, knows his business. To-day is the first time he's ever got wild, and that was probably because he had orders from O'Day.'

'I've never seen that Five Box brand,' said Hashknife. 'What does she look like, Sheriff?'

The sheriff took out the stub of a lead pencil and an envelope. He drew an oblong, three times as long as its width. Across this at right angles he drew another of the same proportions, which made a square centre with the same size squares on each side. It might have been called a cross brand, except that all sides were of equal length.

'That's the Five Box brand,' said the sheriff. 'It was Dutch O'Day's own idea. He said he was goin' to have a brand that nobody could alter and get away with it.'

'It sure looks like he's got it,' grinned Hashknife. ''Most any rustler would baulk

80

at changin' that darned thing. I'd like to meet Dutch O'Day, Sheriff.'

'The hell yuh would! Well, mebby you'll get a chance. We'll see that he comes in for McLeod's hearin', and you'll probably hear him at his very best. He can hate louder and harder than any man on earth.'

'Any special person?' asked Sleepy.

'The one who just spoke to him last.'

Hashknife and Sleepy grinned, and leaned back to let Pat put their orders on the table.

'Yo' no like soup?' asked the Chinaman.

'Compulsory?' grinned Sleepy.

'Jus' same noodle to-day. I hear somebody get kill, eh?'

'Joe Lane and Oscar Naylor,' said the sheriff. 'Two dead men in town to-day, Pat.'

'Shoot each othah, She'iff?'

'No-o-o.'

'Whisky?'

'No-o-o.'

'Hm-m-m! Ve'y solly fo' Joe Lane. Naylor owe me tlee dolla.'

The Chinaman shook his head sadly and shuffled back to the kitchen. He didn't feel sorry for Naylor. He felt sorry for himself, and it would be difficult for another

81

cowboy to get credit at the Pekin Café.

## CHAPTER SIX

# A MEETING AND A FUNERAL

It was two days later that McLeod's hearing was held, and in the meantime the 'Smith brothers' had demonstrated to the poker-playing element of Arapaho City that they knew one card from another.

Corliss offered to take them on at the Five Box ranch, but they declined the jobs. It was all right with Corliss. He had told O'Day about them, and the old Irishman had told him to offer them the customary forty dollars a month.

About fifteen minutes before McLeod's hearing was to take place, Dutch O'Day came to Arapaho City, driving a wild pair of buckskin horses to a buckboard, while beside him sat a big Chinaman, clinging with both hands to the seat.

O'Day drove up in front of the War Paint Saloon, jerked the horses back on their haunches, and swore at the Chinaman for being slow in getting around to their heads.

Hashknife and Sleepy were in front of the saloon, and they were willing to agree with the sheriff's description of O'Day.

He was thin to the point of emaciation, his bony shoulders threatened to tear holes in his colourless shirt, and there was not enough meat on his face to hide the contour of his skull. But his features were typically Irish, and Hashknife wondered if somewhere beneath that wormwood and gall there wasn't a spark of humour and kindness.

'Tie thim up, ye blasted heathen!' he shrilled at the Chinaman, who was fussing with a rope.

He twisted his head and glared at Hashknife and Sleepy.

'Who th' devil are ye starin' at, ye saddle-slickin' dummies?'

'You'd make anybody stare,' said Hashknife coldly. 'I've been told that yo're the meanest man—in this country, but I think they're wrong.

'They didn't cover enough territory, O'Day.'

'Oh!' O'Day leaned back and squinted at Hashknife, his face twisted with impotent wrath. 'Ye don't think they did, eh? If I was able to get out of this rig, I'd pay you

83

out for that.'

'If you'd been able to get out of that rig, somebody would have killed you a year ago. You've gained a sweet reputation, O'Day. Just because yo're a cripple you think you have a right to curse everybody, say what you please. But you haven't. Yo're just a little atom in the scheme of things. Hard luck has soured you, or you think it has, but down in yore soul is the wish that you could come back, that you could have the good will of every one, be a man among men in spite of yore condition.'

O'Day listened to Hashknife, his mouth half open, as if to interrupt. But he held his tongue. The Chinaman finished hitching the team and had come back to the wheel. O'Day shifted his eyes from Hashknife to the Chinaman, squinting at him closely. Then:

'Did ye get thim tied, How Long? Ye did. Thank ye kindly. Now, if ye are ready, How Long, ye may assist me across the way.'

The Chinaman looked curiously at O'Day. It was the first time that O'Day had ever spoken to him in that tone. It had always been with a curse. He leaned inside the buckboard, lifted O'Day easily, and started across the street with him. And O'Day twisted his head, looked back at Hashknife, and actually laughed.

'You see how easy it is, O'Day?' called Hashknife.

The smile snapped out like the turning out of an electric light.

'Go to blazes, will ye?' snarled O'Day, and turned away to swear at How Long.

Hashknife shook his head, still smiling.

'I'm right, Sleepy. O'Day doesn't hate the world. He hates O'Day. He sits at his ranch all the time, knowing that he has made every one dislike him, knowing that no man can speak a good word for him. He can't get out and win back his friends. They won't go to see him. The bitterness of his soul is against himself, and he takes it out on the world.'

'He's sure a perfect cross between a polecat and a badger,' said Sleepy, who was very practical. 'It's too bad the wagon didn't run across his neck.'

There were only three witnesses examined at the hearing—Moon, Corliss, and McLeod. It was a case of two witnesses to one; two men who swore that McLeod opened fire on them without warning, and that it was either the first or second shot

85

that killed Naylor.

McLeod told his story in a straightforward way, but the law accepted the Five Box version, and Scotty McLeod was bound over to the superior court, charged with murder.

Hashknife walked back with McLeod and the sheriff, and when McLeod was again locked in his cell, Hashknife asked him to go over his story again.

'But I've told the truth,' insisted McLeod. 'I can't tell ye any more than I have.'

'What's the idea, Smith?' queried the sheriff.

'I believe McLeod's story, that's all. I hate to see an innocent man sent up or hung. He has told his story. I've heard it twice, but I want to ask questions, if I may.'

'It's all right with me,' said the sheriff. 'I can't make McLeod talk.'

'I'll talk,' nodded the prisoner. 'Ask the questions.'

'How did yore sheep get out?'

'Sure I dunno that.'

'I do. I was out there yesterday. The dead sheep are in the corral, and there's no way for a sheep to get out except through

86

the gate.'

'Ah-ha! So they turned me sheep out, eh?'

'Mebbe.'

'You mean, they wanted an excuse to start trouble with McLeod?' asked the sheriff.

'Somethin' like that. McLeod, you say they were shooting at you as you ran back toward the house?'

'Aye, several shots. I fell into the house, took me gun, fell out through a back window, and went to the corner.'

'Were they still shootin' at the house?'

'Aye, they wer-r-re.'

'They tell me you're a good shot, McLeod. Did you draw a good bead on Naylor?'

'I dunno who he was. Corliss told me that his men were in the hills ready to kill me if I ran back for my gun. I could see some men. I dunno how many. I drew down on one who was on a horse, and I wasn't quite sure of my aim. It was a long ways.'

'And you saw the man fall?'

'I did not. I saw a riderless horse, so I thought I had hit somebody.'

'You didn't know how many men were in

the hills?'

'I did not. I didn't know how many there were until it was all over, and you came with the sheriff.'

'I reckon that's about all,' said Hashknife.

'But that won't help McLeod any,' said the sheriff. 'Even if the Five Box boys did turn the sheep loose to get a reason for startin' trouble, it won't help McLeod much at this trial.'

'Possibly not. But it shows that they intended to start trouble.' Hashknife turned to McLeod. 'Did you ever meet Dutch O'Day?'

'No, I never have. I've minded my own business, and I've had no occasion to go to the Five Box.'

Hashknife and the sheriff went back to the office. The sheriff sighed and sat down in a chair.

'Well, that much of it is over. This afternoon they bury both Naylor and Joe Lane. I was just wonderin''—the sheriff squinted at the ceiling—'just wonderin' what interest you've got in this trouble, Smith?'

Hashknife slowly rolled a cigarette, lighted it carefully, and inhaled deeply before looking at the big sheriff.

'You don't mind, do yuh, Sheriff?'

'Hell, no! But I was just wonderin' if you two happened to drift in here or were yuh sent here. Yuh don't need to answer it either way. Mebby I was thinkin' out loud.'

'We drifted in,' said Hashknife slowly. 'Mebby there was a reason, but nobody sent us. A week ago we didn't know anythin' about the Twisted River country.'

'Yore business is yore own,' said the sheriff. 'Excuse me for talkin' about it. Are yuh goin' to the funerals?'

'Nope. We didn't know either of 'em. And we're not morbidly curious.'

'I reckon yo're right. I've got to go. Folks are talkin' about me and my rustlin' deputy, and I've got to stick with him to the last sod.'

'You don't think the old man killed him on purpose, knew who he was, do yuh?'

'My God, no! If you could have seen the look on the old man's face when he seen it was Joe Lane! No, Hank Ludden is no murderer. I'd bank on it, Smith.'

Hashknife left the office and wandered up the street. Old Dutch O'Day was sitting in his buckboard, talking with Corliss. Hashknife saw them look towards him and

89

exchange a few words. Then Corliss nodded his head and walked towards the door of the War Paint Saloon.

Hashknife intended to ignore O'Day, but O'Day would have it otherwise, and called to Hashknife.

'How's yore disposition?' asked Hashknife.

'What do you care?' retorted O'Day.

'I just wanted to know before I stopped, O'Day. I might throw a rock at a peevish old badger, but I'd not stop and waste words with him.'

'Come back here!' snapped O'Day. 'You're the first damn' man I've seen in a year that had guts enough to tell me where to head in.' Hashknife came back and leaned against a front wheel.

'Corliss offered ye a job, didn't he?' asked O'Day.

'Yeah,' indifferently.

'Mebbe ye don't want a job.'

'Mebbe not.'

'Ah-h-h-h-h!' O'Day cleared his throat angrily. 'Ye'r too damn' cool! That damn' heathen pair o' legs of mine has gone down to the Pekin Café to ta-alk Chinese wid another of the same breed, and I'm left here to the mercy of every gallinipper that—

that—' O'Day spat viciously and glared at Hashknife.

'Why don'tcha smile for a change?' asked Hashknife. 'I'd be a little careful at first, if I was you, 'cause it'll wrinkle yore face the other way and might break the skin.'

O'Day glared with impotent wrath, his hands clenched in his lap. But as Hashknife had surmised, back of his bitterness was a spark of humour, and it was forced to the surface.

'Ye almost made me laugh,' he said, choking a trifle.

'I'm not tryin' to make yuh laugh. I'm tryin' to make yuh think, O'Day.'

'Think?' O'Day stared at him and his face twisted with bitterness. 'My God, man, what do ye think I've been doin' since I lost me legs? Think? Ha, ha, ha, ha! That's all there is left for me to do—think.'

Hashknife turned his head and looked at Hank Ludden and Armadillo Jones, who were crossing the street from a hitch-rack.

'I'd rather be in your fix than in Hank Ludden's,' said Hashknife softly.

'Ye'd rather? And why would ye, man?'

'He killed his daughter's husband.'

'I know he did. Joe Lane was a rustler.'

'No matter what he was, O'Day; they say

91

that Ludden worshipped his daughter. She married against his wishes and he has never been to see her. She loved her husband enough to give up her father, and he killed her husband. Ain't that worse than not bein' able to walk? Yore pain was physical, O'Day. Any ache in yore soul has been put there willingly by you.'

O'Day turned his head and looked at Ludden, squinting thoughtfully. Then he turned back and nodded.

'Perhaps you're right,' he said slowly. 'God knows I've hurt no one except with my tongue. I wonder does the man realize what he has done.'

'I think so, O'Day. I watched his face the other day when his daughter passed him by. I felt the pain in it myself, and I'm kinda salty. And the pain won't pass like the pain of a physical hurt. But I don't think he'll curse the world for something that he can't help.'

'Here comes my Chinese legs,' said O'Day softly. 'I hope he had a good visit with Pat Ling.'

The big Chinaman came up to them, looking inquiringly at O'Day, waiting for his orders.

'We'll be going, How Long,' said

O'Day, and then to Hashknife: 'If ye care to, come out to the Five Box, Smith. If ye need a job for you or your pardner, come and get it. I'm glad I stopped ye when I did. So-long.'

Hashknife stepped closer and held out his hand. O'Day hesitated, glanced around, as though wondering who might see it, and grasped Hashknife's hand.

'The first handshake in years,' he said huskily. 'Perhaps it's because ye are a stranger. No, by God! Ye knew what I am—was—and ye—' O'Day turned to the Chinaman. 'Don't drive too fast, How Long. Me legs are hur-rtin' me.'

Without another glance at Hashknife, O'Day drove away. As far as Hashknife could see them, O'Day had not turned his head. Hashknife stepped on the sidewalk in front of the saloon and leaned against a post, rolling a cigarette.

Arapaho City was getting ready for the double funeral. Down in front of the livery stable a man was washing the antiquated hearse, its two remaining black plumes standing askew on opposite corners of the equipage. As Hashknife watched the cleaner, another man brought out two grey horses which they proceeded to hitch to the hearse.

Several men were going around the old cottonwood heading for the doctor's home where the services were to be held. Rigs were arriving regularly, but were turning off to the right before reaching the main street.

Across the street from Hashknife, sitting close together on a bench, were Hank Ludden and Armadillo Jones. The proprietor of the general store came out, wearing his cutaway coat and an antiquated derby hat. He locked the door, glanced quickly at the two men on the bench, and hurried up the street.

★　　★　　★

The hearse went past, rattling badly from disuse, the two grey horses swinging away from each other as the driver checked their natural tendencies to go fast. The two old men watched the hearse turn the corner, but it seemed to Hashknife that neither of them spoke to the other.

Sleepy came from the saloon with Honey Moon and Corliss, followed by Dayne—a skinny, bowlegged cowboy who carried his left arm stiffly bent at the elbow, as though

about to strike at something or somebody.
His nose had been broken at some time,
giving him a disc-faced appearance.

'Goin' to the funeral, Smith?' asked
Corliss.

Hashknife shook his head.

'Nope, I'm not curious.'

'I ain't goin' either,' said Sleepy.

'We've kinda got to go,' said Honey
Moon dolefully. 'Yuh see, Naylor ain't got
no relation, not that we know about, and it
ain't a reg'lar funeral unless somebody
mourns. Naylor was a good feller and he
deserves a send-off.'

'C'mon,' grunted Dayne. 'Let's git it
over with. I'm glad Dutch O'Day didn't
decide to go to the funeral. He'd likely cuss
the minister before it was over with.'

The three cowboys went down the
sidewalk rattling their spurs, mounted their
horses at the hitch-rack, and rode around
the corner. The sheriff came up the
opposite side of the street until he noticed
the two old men on the bench, when he
crossed the street and came up to
Hashknife and Sleepy.

'I didn't want to pass 'em,' he told
Hashknife. 'I got close enough to see old
Hank's face, and that was enough for me.'

'I guess that's right,' nodded Hashknife.

'Well'—the sheriff sighed deeply—'I reckon I've got to go and set on the mourners' bench, boys. These things ain't so easy for me.'

'You won't be on the mourners' bench,' said Hashknife. 'It's over there in front of the store.'

'I reckon yo're right at that. So-long.'

The sheriff went on, his Sunday boots creaking a protest. Hashknife rolled a fresh cigarette, his expression deadly serious as he spread the tobacco carefully along the crimped paper. Sleepy glanced at him and began rolling one for himself.

'I'm ready,' said Sleepy seriously, 'to add my quit-claim deed to that other one on the Arapaho City signboard. Anybody can have my share of the damn' thing.'

Hashknife shook his head, squinting thoughtfully, the unlighted cigarette hanging to his lower lip. Slowly he drew a match from his pocket and snapped it to a light with his thumbnail.

'We can't leave now, Sleepy. I can't go away and remember them two old men over on that bench, and that white-faced woman. I'd always be lookin' back, wonderin', you know, Sleepy.'

'Yeah, I know, cowboy.'

'And there a letter I've got to answer.'

'When?'

'Just as soon as I find his address.'

Sleepy nodded and hitched up his belt, indicating the saloon door with a jerk of his head.

'All right,' said Hashknife. 'I need one just now.'

They went into the War Paint. There were only two human beings left on the main street of Arapaho City: two old men who humped together on the little bench, straining their eyes towards a spot beyond the old cottonwood where they could see the first few rigs of the funeral procession lining up for the cemetery trip.

## CHAPTER SEVEN

# ON THE TRAIL OF CLUES

The next day Hashknife and Sleepy rode out to the old U6 corral. The sheriff had given them directions, and they had little trouble in finding the place, as an old road, nearly grown up with weeds and brush, led from the main highway to where the old ranch-house once stood.

A few Five Box and HL cattle were at the old waterhole, and a magpie chattered at them from a high pole of the corral. They drew up beside the old fence and Hashknife glanced at his watch.

'It took us almost an hour to reach here, Sleepy,' he remarked.

'That's prob'ly a world's record,' said Sleepy dryly. 'What'll we do now? Go back to Arapaho and brag about it?'

Hashknife replaced his watch and ignored Sleepy's sarcasm.

'All right, I'll give us three cheers,' grinned Sleepy.

They went around to the corral gate, looking for evidences of the branding-fire, but there were none.

'Tracked out or wiped out,' said Hashknife.

He squinted at the top of the ridge from where Hank Ludden had first seen the rustlers at work.

'That must be where the old man's horse came out and put the rustlers on the run,' said Hashknife. 'It's too bad he came alone after them.'

'It's too bad he came at all,' replied

Sleepy. 'He'd 'a' saved himself a lot of misery by stayin' home that day. What'll we do next?'

'From what the sheriff said, the HL Ranch must lie almost due north of here. So we'll kinda angle out through the hills and visit old man Ludden. I'd like to have a little talk with him.'

They circled to the left of the butte and headed north, riding slowly. After the first mile the hills were more open, covered with a fairly good growth of bunch-grass and dotted here and there with live-oaks, the creek bottoms heavy with cottonwoods and a few sycamores.

Cattle grazed on the open slopes of the hills, stopping their feeding to gaze with deep suspicion upon the two riders. In each group there seemed to be one or two more suspicious than the others, and these would start running away, followed by the rest.

'There's a lot more Five Box than HL's,' observed Hashknife as they skirted the side of the bunch-grass hill. They came out on the crest and drew up to scan the country to the eastward.

They were high enough up to locate Arapaho City and to see the hills behind Scotty McLeod's place. Between them and

Arapaho City was the green, snake-like line of Twisted River which swung in south-east, passing close to the Five Box Ranch.

They rode down the ridge, crossing the head of a deep canyon, and came out on a flat mesa which led them out to a view of the Hard Luck Ranch far down in the mouth of the little valley, its elevated position making it plainly visible.

Hashknife led the way, following the higher ground until they struck the slope which led down to the ranchhouse. Old Armadillo was in the yard greasing a buckboard. He had a smear of axle grease on his chin, and his hands were gobby from the same substance in spite of the fact that he was using a stick to apply it to the axle.

He paid no attention to their approach and did not look up until several moments after they had stopped beside him. Then he straightened up, placed the grease can and stick in the buckboard, and felt tenderly of his back.

'Gittin' so old that I squeak,' he said. 'Been puttin' off greasin' that dinged e-qui-page f'r a long time, jist 'cause it creaks m' back. Gittin' old, I reckon. Gittin' old jist like that damn' buckboard. But nobody can grease me and take out the squeaks.

'Well, are yuh goin' to set there or are yuh goin' to git down and give them horses a rest? Yore names are Smith, and yo're brothers. Howdy. I'm Armadillo Jones, meaner'n hell and as dangerous as a sage-rabbit.'

The two cowboys dismounted and shook hands gravely with Armadillo, trying not to laugh. Then he handed them a rag to wipe their greasy hands with, and they all laughed.

'Where's Ludden?' asked Hashknife.

'Hank? He's up at the house, settin' there.' Armadillo spoke the last two words softly and looked towards the house.

'You know about it, don'tcha?' he asked.

'Yeah, we know about it,' said Hashknife.

'Uh-huh,' thoughtfully. 'Well, I dunno. Hank was younger'n me before this happened, but right now I'm a yearlin' beside him. Don't want nothin' to drink nor eat—jist sets.'

'Hit him hard, eh?'

'Jist like a ton of brick with a muzzle ve-locity of ten thousand feet per second. Wait'll I hook that damn' wheel on and I'll go up with yuh. Mebby it'll do him good to hear a strange voice.'

101

Hashknife helped him put on the wheel and they went to the front of the house, where they found Ludden sitting on the porch, slumped down in a chair, a dead pipe between his lips. He turned his head and looked at Hashknife and Sleepy.

'Hank, these here are a couple of Smiths,' said Armadillo. 'Gents, I make yuh used to Hank Ludden.'

'Don't get up,' said Hashknife, holding out his hand.

Ludden shook hands listlessly and waited for them to say what they wanted of him. Armadillo scowled at Ludden.

'Well, good God, Hank!' he blurted. 'This ain't no way to meet anybody. Shake yoreself, can'tcha?'

'Please don't, Armadillo,' replied Ludden. 'I—I reckon I was half asleep when yuh came up—dreamin'.'

'That's all right,' smiled Hashknife. 'We just dropped in to say howdy and see how things are goin'.'

'To see how things are goin'?'

'I can tell yuh they ain't goin' worth a damn,' said Armadillo.

'Shucks, that's no way to look at it,' grinned Hashknife. 'Remember that every cloud has a silver linin'.'

102

Hank Ludden turned quickly.

'Not every cloud. Not some clouds that I know, Smithy.'

'Let's forget the clouds for a while, Ludden. Did you ever hear of a man named Hashknife Hartley?'

'Hashknife Hartley? Why, I—I—'

'Yo're right yuh did!' snorted Armadillo. 'Last spring yuh—'

'Yes, I knew of a man by that name. I wrote him a letter. But what has that to do—'

'You wrote to him at Calumet?' interrupted Hashknife.

'Yes, that was the town.'

'It's funny I didn't get it. We just left there a short time ago.'

'Nothin' funny about it,' said Armadillo. 'Hank wrote on the envelope, "After ten days return to Hank Ludden, Arapaho City," and that's what they done.'

'Are you Hashknife Hartley?' asked Ludden.

'That's me.'

'H'm-m-m-m.' Ludden stared at him closely. 'Then if you didn't get that letter, how did yuh know I wrote to yuh?'

'Mebby I'm a mind-reader,' smiled Hashknife. He did not want to tell them about the other letter.

'I don't believe it!' snapped Armadillo. 'No damn' man read yore mind. But,' he added seriously, 'that kinda fits in with what Amos Hardy told yuh, Hank. He said that Hashknife Hartley was worse'n a palmist when it comes to puttin' the deadwood on a rustler or a killer.'

'Amos Hardy, eh?' Hashknife smiled. He knew Amos, the big roly-poly cattle-buyer for an Eastern packing house.

'Know him, don'tcha?' asked Armadillo.

'Yeah, I know Amos. But we haven't seen him for over a year. It seems to me that you wanted me to come out and take charge of the HL Ranch.'

'Did we?' Ludden's teeth gripped tightly on his pipe-stem. 'If you didn't read my letter, how in hell did yuh know what we wanted?'

'Mind-readin',' drawled Armadillo dryly.

'Hardy told him,' declared Ludden.

'We haven't seen him for over a year,' reminded Hashknife.

'Mind-readin',' reiterated Armadillo. 'But what difference does it make how he found out, Hank? We're in a damn' sight worse hole than we was in April.'

'No one was ever in a worse hole,' gloomed Ludden.

'Job had boils and the whale swallered Jonah,' offered Hashknife seriously, and Armadillo laughed.

'Yuh can draw a boil to a head, and I never did believe that whale yarn no more'n I believe yo're a mind-reader. It ain't none of my business how yuh found out that Hank wrote yuh a letter last spring, and I don't give a damn.'

'That's the spirit,' grinned Hashknife. 'Where was yuh when Amos Hardy told yuh so much about me?'

'Right here on this porch.'

'Thasso? Who was present?'

'Me and Hank and Hardy.'

'Nobody else heard what he said, eh?'

'Not a soul.'

'Hardy came alone,' nodded Ludden.

'Is Hardy well known around here?'

'Ought to be.' Thus Armadillo. 'He's been buyin' beef in the Twisted River country f'r years. Shows up about twice a year.'

'Any other buyers?'

'Hell, yes! But Amos is so well known that he gets what he wants. He used to buy quite a lot from us, but lately we ain't sold none.'

'And a damn' good reason for not sellin',' added Ludden.

'Where do yuh ship from—when yuh ship?'

'Casco. We have to drive twenty miles to a railroad. It's all good travellin'. They've been sayin' that a branch is to be built in Arapaho, but I don't reckon it ever will. The railroad intended to come in thisaway, but they couldn't get out of this pocket without goin' out through Crow Rock Canyon, and that'd cost a lot of money. So they swings to the east from Casco and misses this spur of the Twisted River Mountains.'

'What towns are between here and Casco?'

'Bend and Lone Tree. It's about eight miles to Bend, five from Bend to Lone Tree, and about seven from there to Casco.'

'Cattle raised all up the valley?'

'Yeah. Little alfalfa raised, but mostly stock. All small outfits, the JME, K8, 103, Box X, Diamond Z, and 7 Bar 9.'

Hashknife drew out pencil and paper and asked Ludden to enumerate the brands again, while he drew them out on the back of an envelope.

'I told yuh in my letter that I wanted yuh to take charge of the HL,' said Ludden earnestly. 'That still holds good.'

'This proposition has gone past that stage,' replied Hashknife, pocketing his envelope. 'You need a man at large, not in charge. Has anythin' ever happened to cause yuh to think that Joe Lane was a rustler?'

Ludden sighed heavily and shook his head.

'No, Hartley. It was an awful shock to me. I don't reckon I'll ever get over it. I know I'll never notch a sight on another human bein'. They can steal all my cows if they want to.'

'By God, they can't steal mine!' snorted Armadillo. 'I could pot-shot the rest of the world and never hit a relation of mine. Ain't got none. Paw said he was the last bud on the fambly tree, and he married an orphing. I'm the result, Armadillo Jones, meaner'n hell!'

'What will yore daughter do now?' asked Hashknife of Ludden.

'God only knows. They ain't got much. Joe's salary was enough to keep 'em, but there's no salary now. I dunno what she'll do, Hartley.'

'Couldn't yuh induce her to come back here?'

'Here?' snorted Armadillo. 'Why, she won't even speak to us!'

'She'd be welcome, wouldn't she?'

'Welcome?' Armadillo pronounced the word softly and looked at Ludden. 'Jist like rain is welcome in July when the whole range smokes from the heat—when the water-holes are all dry and the cottonwood leaves curl up on the tree. That's jist how welcome she'd be at the HL.'

'That's welcome enough,' said Hashknife. 'We'll mosey on back to town, I reckon.'

Armadillo urged them to spend the rest of the day and have supper with them at the HL, but Hashknife explained that he was too busy to attend social functions. 'Social hell!' snorted Armadillo. 'Don't let that part of it stand in yore road.'

'I dunno what there is for yuh to do,' complained Ludden. 'I killed Joe Lane for stealin' cattle, and there ain't enough HL cattle left to make much difference. There's two rustlers left, and they'll be smart enough to keep quiet for a while.'

★      ★      ★

Sleepy argued that side of the case with Hashknife as they rode back to Arapaho City, but got little satisfaction out of it. Hashknife had told Sleepy about his conversation with Dutch O'Day, and their talk drifted to Scotty McLeod.

'They'll sure send him over the road,' declared Sleepy. 'A cattle jury won't give him a chance, and that's the kind of jury they'll draw here. Somebody was sayin' that Lane and McLeod were pretty good friends.'

'Thasso?' Hashknife squinted thoughtfully. 'Huh! I wonder if—'

Hashknife squinted at the sun, estimating the time of day. Perhaps it was easier than taking out his watch.

'Wonder if what?' queried Sleepy.

'Just wonderin'.'

They rode across the rickety old bridge over Twisted River, and were almost to Arapaho City when they met the sheriff.

'I was just goin' out to the HL,' he told them. 'Got tired of settin' around and thought I'd go out and talk with Hank and Armadillo a while.'

'We just came from there,' said Hashknife. 'I was thinkin' about ridin' over to McLeod's place and takin' a look around.'

'Yeah? McLeod's place, eh? Wasn't yuh out there day before yesterday?'

'Uh-huh. But I didn't go in the house.'

'Didn't yuh? Hm-m-m-m. What do yuh expect to find in there?'

'Nothin'.'

The sheriff shifted in his saddle and spat reflectively.

'Nothin', eh?' he mused, his keen eyes searching Hashknife's lean features. Then—

'Smith, who are you, anyway?'

'One of the Smith brothers,' seriously.

'Cripes!' The sheriff expressed his disbelief explosively. 'Names don't mean nothin'. You ride in here on a wave of crime, turn down jobs, help me take a man, and then go pokin' around like a danged detective lookin' for a clue. Mebby yo're just the Smith brothers, I dunno. But I just don't mind tellin' yuh that I ain't the only one in Arapaho City who wonders who in hell yuh are.'

Hashknife grinned and produced the makings of a cigarette.

'Smith is. as good a name as any,' he said slowly. 'Our own names won't mean

110

anythin' to yuh, Darcey. Nobody sent us here, nobody is payin' us for what we're doin'. We're just what we look like—two driftin' punchers.

'We busted in on two killin's. Nobody can tell us what we want to know, so we go huntin' for the answer. If we find it, we'll let yuh know. If we get killed, it's our own fault.'

'Fair enough,' nodded Darcey. 'If yuh don't care, I'll ride to the McLeod place with yuh. But if yuh think yuh can clear McLeod, you've got a job on yore hands.'

'I hadn't thought much about it,' grinned Hashknife. 'Was Joe Lane friendly with McLeod?'

'Well, yeah. McLeod is a likeable Scotchman if yuh don't rub him the wrong way. Joe liked him. Mcleod has travelled quite a lot and Joe liked to talk with him. But what does that mean?'

'If Joe Lane stole cows, he didn't do it alone.'

'Oh-ho! And yuh think—I see. But there was three of 'em.'

'Mebby we can find out who the third one was, Sheriff.'

'Mebbe,' hopefully.

They turned to the right near Arapaho

111

City and cut across the hills to Mcleod's cabin. No one had bothered to bury the sheep, and the odours were none too inviting.

The cabin doors were unlocked, swinging half open. They went in and looked around. Most of McLeod's few belongings were in the rear part of the building. His bed had been carefully made.

On the rough table a million ants were making merry with an open can of syrup, and the top of the stove was covered with coffee-grounds from the last brewing which Scotty had been forced to ignore.

There was no furniture to speak of. And old trunk with a broken lock, covered with an Indian blanket, stood near the head of the bed, used as a table. Hanging on nails near the head of the bed was a well-worn pair of overalls, an old black coat, and a battered sombrero hat.

Hashknife walked around the room, examining things, while the sheriff and Sleepy watched him. He lifted the lid of the old trunk and examined the few things within it: a grey coat and vest, a nearly new pair of boots, some old odds and ends of wearing apparel.

Hashknife closed the trunk, and lifted

the old black coat off the nail. In the inside pocket he found a miscellaneous bunch of old letters, bearing British stamps. Hashknife did not read these letters. But among the envelopes was a folded sheet of paper, which almost escaped his eye.

He unfolded this and scanned the short pencilled note, which read:

Have them thear at east end of Crow Rock canyon next Friday sure don't try to run as menny as last time and go easy.

Hashknife smiled softly and handed the paper to the sheriff, who read it blankly, while Sleepy looked over his shoulder.

'What do yuh make of it?' asked the sheriff.

'Hey!' snorted Sleepy. 'Ain't that the same writin' as in that letter you got, Hashknife?'

Hashknife laughed and nodded his head. The sheriff looked gravely at Hashknife and handed back the note.

'So that's yore name, eh? Hashknife Hartley?'

'I didn't suppose you'd ever heard of me,' said Hashknife.

'I have. Yuh see, I've been a sheriff for

almost four years, and we do hear things once in a while. Was you sent here by the cattle association?'

'Nope.' Hashknife drew out the letter he had received in Calumet and handed it to the sheriff.

'Compare the writin',' suggested Sleepy—which they found to be identical. The sheriff read the letter and listened as Hashknife told him about Hank Ludden's returned letter. The one he received, of course, had no return address.

Then Hashknife told him that Amos Hardy had suggested to Ludden that he get in touch with Hashknife Hartley.

'Well,' said the sheriff gravely, 'I'm glad yuh came. But you better not tell anybody who yuh are, Hartley. This letter sure is a warnin' that yuh can't disregard.'

'It didn't scare me much. The man who wrote me that letter ain't never quit lookin' for me to show up here, and I'll bet he knows who I am right now.'

'Do yuh think so? Huh. Who do yuh think wrote it?'

'That remains to be found out. How far is it from here to Crow Rock Canyon?'

'About three miles. The canyon cuts plumb through the range, and it's about

114

two miles through. Do yuh reckon this letter was Scotty McLeod's instructions on movin' cattle?'

'Can yuh think of anythin' else he might take through the canyon? It tells him to not run as many as before and to go easy. Must be somebody over there who takes 'em off his hands.'

'Sure,' nodded the sheriff. 'It ain't far from the east end of the canyon to McCallville. I'll betcha Scotty runs a bunch through the canyon at night, turns 'em over to somebody at the other end and they handle 'em from McCallville.'

'And to-day is Thursday,' mused Hashknife. 'This letter tells him to have 'em there on Friday. The question is, what Friday did he mean? Is it to-morrow or was it last Friday, two, three, four weeks ago to-morrow? No date on the letter, nothin' to show when the cattle were to be moved.'

'Makes it kinda tough,' agreed the sheriff. 'But it sure puts McLeod up against some hard travellin'. He'll have a hard time explainin' away that note.'

'McLeod says he had been to town the mornin' that Lane was killed. He told us about that part of it, Sheriff. If he can prove that much, it'll help him. A man can't be in two places at the same time.'

'Not if it can be proved, Hartley. But you know it would only take about forty minutes for a man to make the ride from Arapaho City to the old U6 corral. McLeod won't be able to find a man who can swear within an hour of the time he was in Arapaho, because his being there wouldn't be of enough interest for any one to make a note of it.'

'Is there any one who can swear what time Joe Lane left Arapaho City and where he intended to go?'

'Joe told me he was goin' out to the Five Box Ranch to look at a horse. One of the boys out there has a three-year-old sorrel that Joe liked, and Joe wanted to buy it. But I've no idea what time Joe left town.

'His time was mostly his own. I never pinned Joe down to regular hours. I have no home, so I spend most of my time at the office. He was usually where I could find him.'

'Did he ever talk much about the rustlers?'

'No more than the rest of us did, Hartley.'

'How did he feel toward Hank Ludden?'

'He felt that the old man had too much

sense to stay mad all his life. Joe didn't hate Ludden. At least, he never seemed to. He wanted Ludden to be friends with Mary, because he knew it hurt Mary for the old man to feel as he did. Joe liked old Armadillo Jones, meaner'n hell.'

The sheriff laughed as he quoted Armadillo's description of himself. Hashknife grinned and walked to the door, where he examined a bullet-scrape along the casing. Then he crossed the room, took out his pocket-knife, and dug out a battered thirty-thirty bullet which had barely buried itself in a seasoned board.

'Thirty-thirty,' said Hashknife, tossing the bullet to the sheriff. 'McLeod swore they were shootin' at him as he ran for that back door. It kinds looks like he might have told the truth.'

Hashknife went outside and looked for more evidence. In the doorstep was another bullet-hole, and in the doorframe was embedded a pebble the size of a small marble, which might have been driven in by a bullet striking the ground short of the door.

He showed these to the sheriff, who nodded gravely.

'It looks like McLeod told the truth,' he

admitted. 'But how would a jury look at it, Hartley? There's nothin' to prove when those shots were fired. It might have been months ago.'

'No, that's right. Well, we might as well go home.'

The sheriff secured some nails and fastened the doors tight. There was nothing in the place which might tempt a thief, but the sheriff thought it would look better to have the doors nailed shut.

Back at their room in the Arapaho Hotel, Hashknife stretched himself full length on the bed and stared at the ceiling, while Sleepy proceeded to play solitaire with an old dog-eared deck of cards on the little table.

For an hour there was no conversation, no sound except the soft riffling as Sleepy shuffled the cards or when Hashknife moved sightly, causing the bed to creak. Then Hashknife said aloud:

'We can get to the east end before dark.'

'East end of what?' Sleepy lifted his head quickly.

'Crow Rock Canyon.'

'Oh, yeah.'

'We'll borrow a couple of rifles from the sheriff. Put up them cards, cowboy.'

Hashknife twisted off the bed and reached for his hat.

'If anybody brings a cow through that canyon, we'll be there to welcome 'em, Sleepy.'

'Friday jist means to-morrow to you, does it?' wailed Sleepy.

'We can't be there last Friday,' retorted Hashknife.

The sheriff was willing to lend them the guns and ammunition, and insisted on going along, but Hashknife persuaded him to stay at home.

'It's a hundred-to-one shot that we don't see anybody,' said Hashknife. 'If there's a man over there to receive the stock, he's prob'ly heard that McLeod is in jail, so we'll have our trouble for nothin'. If there is a man there—well, two of us will be as good as an army.'

Crow Rock Canyon was visible from Arapaho City, and the sheriff gave them directions as to the easiest way to reach the west end of it. They had Pat, the chinaman, make them each a sandwich, which they tied inside their slickers, purchased some extra cartridges for their thirty-thirty rifles, and rode out of town.

# CHAPTER EIGHT

## A VERY LIVE WIRE

Mary Lane had just begun to recover from the shock of losing her husband, and the cold, hard facts of existence were staring her in the face. It had just occurred to her that she had no visible means of support, except her father.

Joe had not been of a saving disposition. She did not know how much money there was in the bank in his name, but she did not imagine it to be any great amount. Joe's last month's salary had paid for the funeral, leaving her a few dollars extra.

She had tried to forgive her father for what he had done, but found it impossible to do so. He had shot Joe for a rustler, and Mary would gamble her soul that Joe had been honest.

To her it seemed that her father had merely used this as an excuse to kill Joe.

'And I'm the wife, the widow of a dead thief,' she told herself bitterly. 'That's what they say about me. He shot Joe in the back. Never gave him a chance.'

She stared at herself in the mirror; stared at her own white face with the dark-circled eyes, as if she were looking at someone she had never seen. A few days had changed her from a laughter-loving girl to a tragic-faced woman.

She hated to leave the house, to be seen on the street. None of her old friends had been to see her, and she knew it was because Joe had been labelled a rustler. An officer of the law, a thief!

Her mind only ran in circles when she tried to plan a future. But she had a definite idea of leaving Arapaho City. Just where she might go or what she might do was indefinite. Much depended on how many dollars Joe had left for her.

It was shortly after Hashknife and Sleepy had ridden out of town that she came to the bank. Dutch O'Day and Long How had just driven in and were stopped in front of the bank. The little wizen-faced Irishman squinted closely at Mary as she walked past, going into the bank.

Long How went in, spoke to the president of the bank, who came out to him. O'Day's account was worth a certain amount of service. He had come in to draw cash enough for his payroll. It was the first time he had ever talked with the president of the bank without cursing someone.

The president went in after the required money, and it was several minutes later that he came out with it. He seemed preoccupied. Through the open door O'Day had seen him in conversation with Mary Lane.

As he went back, Mary Lane came out. She stood on the threshold of the bank, deep in thought.

'How do ye do, Mrs. Lane,' said O'Day abruptly.

She looked up quickly. It was the first time he had ever spoken to her, although she had known him for years.

'Quite well, thank you, Mr. O'Day,' she said, hardly realizing that she had answered him.

'Ye're not!' he declared. 'Don't fib about it.'

Mary Lane almost laughed. It seemed ridiculous for Dutch O'Day, the meanest man in the Twisted River country, to talk so to her. He was smiling at her, and she remembered that O'Day never smiled.

'No, ye're not all right,' he told her. 'Come over closer to me, Mary Lane. Ye see, I can't come to you.'

She came closer, wonderingly.

'I'm sorry,' she said.

'For me?'

'Yes, Mr. O'Day.'

O'Day rubbed his chin and blinked thoughtfully.

'Did Joe leave ye any money?' he asked.

Mary shook her head.

'I'm afraid he—he didn't have much to leave.'

'No, I suppose not. Will ye go back to yer father?'

Mary stared at him for a moment and shook her head.

'No,' she said.

'Ye haven't talked with him?'

'No.'

'Hm-m-m-m.' O'Day cleared his throat raspingly. 'Mary Lane, I dunno just what to say. Ye see, I'—he rubbed his chin violently—'I was just thinkin' that—well—it—here ye are:

'The Five Box has no women. We're a rough lot out there. But if ye want a home, I'll give it to ye. I've plenty, and I've no chick or child to spend it on.'

'Oh, that is awfully good of you, Mr. O'Day,' said Mary, and she meant it now. She had ceased to be astonished at O'Day.

'But I couldn't do that. I can get along some way. But I want you to know I appreciate your kindness.'

'I know, Mary Lane. Only don't forget that the offer still stands as long as ye might need it.'

He turned abruptly, picked up the lines, and swung the team out into the street, leaving her there staring after him. He drew the team to a stop in front of the sheriff's office and spoke to Long How, who grinned, got out, and went towards the Pekin Café, glad for a chance to talk with one of his own race.

O'Day squinted back up the street. Mary Lane was turning the corner, going home.

The sheriff came to his doorway and nodded to O'Day. They had never been good friends because of O'Day's vitriolic tongue.

'How is everything, Pete?' asked O'Day kindly.

'All right, O'Day. How is everythin' with you?'

'Fine. I was just talkin' with Mary Lane, Pete. She's up against a tough deal. Joe left her little or no money, I suppose.'

It rather shocked the sheriff to hear O'Day speaking of other people's troubles.

He wondered if O'Day was sick or had gone crazy.

'Well, I don't suppose Joe did leave much,' admitted the sheriff slowly. 'In fact, I don't reckon he left anythin'.'

'Ye know damn' well he didn't!' It was a return of the old Dutch O'Day. 'These damn' young fools git married and—but'— he squinted at the sheriff and grinned widely—'we were all young once, Pete Darcey. If they'd killed me in me twenties, I'd have left nothin'.'

'It's the nature of humanity,' said the sheriff, wondering at the sudden change in the man.

'What salary did Joe Lane get from this county, Pete?'

'Hundred and ten dollars a month,' replied the sheriff.

'And he still has about fourteen months left of your two-year term. Hm-m-n. Have ye an indilible pencil, Pete?'

Wonderingly the sheriff gave him the required article, and watched O'Day take out his cheque book and begin to write.

He finished the cheque and looked up at the sheriff.

'There's no chance of gettin' the county to pay anything to the widow of a dead deputy, is there?' he asked.

'Hardly. Perhaps if he had been killed in upholdin' the law, O'Day. But Joe wasn't.'

'To hell wid the law! The man is dead, ain't he? His widow never stole any cows. Here, Pete.'

He handed the sheriff a cheque for fifteen hundred dollars. 'Put that in the bank and pay her a hundred and ten dollars every month.'

'But she won't take it, O'Day. You don't know her.'

'Tell her that the kind-hearted county paid it to her, Pete. She can't refuse it then. Keep my name out of it. Tell her not to say anything about it, 'cause the county don't want it generally known. Ye're workin' for a kind-hearted county, and ye don't know it.'

The sheriff looked at the cheque and squinted at O'Day.

'Dutch O'Day,' he said slowly, 'what in blazes happened to you?'

'None of yer damn' business, Pete Darcey! It's me own money and I can do what I like wid it, can't I? But if I hear that you ever told anybody about that cheque, I'll ride ye down the first time I catch ye in the street.'

126

'And I'll stand still and let yuh, O'Day. Just now I'd like to shake hands with yuh.'

The big muscular hand of the sheriff enveloped the scrawny brown hand of O'Day, the meanest man in the Twisted River country, and they shook gravely. Then O'Day drove down to the Pekin Café, where he humped over in his seat to wait until Long How got through talking with Pat Lee, the other Chinaman of Arapaho.

The sheriff went into his office, spread the cheque out on his desk, and sat down to try and figure out what had happened to Dutch O'Day to cause him to give away fifteen hundred dollars to someone he did not even have a speaking acquaintance with.

But the sheriff was unable to arrive at any logical conclusion except that possibly Dutch O'Day had a hunch he was going to die, and wanted to spend some of his money. Anyway, he decided, it was a fine thing for O'Day to do, and there was no question of Mary Lane's need.

He decided to bank the money and tell Mary that the county had ordered the bank to issue her a monthly allowance instead of having the county treasurer issue the usual voucher cheque.

So he picked up his hat and went to the bank. It was just at closing time, but the cashier was willing to delay his departure to accommodate the sheriff.

'Here's a cheque for fifteen hundred dollars,' stated the sheriff, producing the slip of pink paper. 'You credit that to the account of Mary Lane, and give her one hundred and ten dollars a month as long as it lasts.'

The cashier looked at the cheque, nodding his head as he turned back to his desk.

'You merely want us to issue that amount per month, eh? No explantion needed, I suppose?'

'I'll explain to her.'

He wrote out a receipt and gave it to the sheriff, who went outside and started for the office, meeting Armadillo Jones.

'Yo're the feller I want to see,' grinned Armadillo. 'You know how the county does things, Pete. Listen t'me, feller. I'm danged if I was goin' to see Mary Lane starve, *sabe?* So I went to the bank awhile ago, drawed fifteen hundred dollars of my own money, handed it back to 'em, and fixed it up so's they'll pay Mary one hundred and ten dollars per month for the rest of Joe's unexpired term.

'I fixed it up for them to tell her that the county was payin' her Joe's salary, but for her to keep quiet about it, as it was kinda irregular.'

Armadillo laughed softly and shuffled his feet.

'I didn't let Hank know a danged thing about it. Anyway, it's my money and I can do as I damn' please with it. I got away from Hank, and it didn't take me long to fix things. Ha, ha, ha, ha! Pretty good, eh?'

The sheriff tried to grin, but failed.

'Yeah, that was pretty good, Armadillo. She—uh—sure needs the money.'

'Sure thing. But here's what I want you to do, Pete. If she knowed it was from the HL outfit, mebby she wouldn't take it. So I want you to kinda let on that there's a chance of the county payin' her sort of a pension. Will yuh do this?'

'Eh? Oh, sure.' The sheriff rubbed his chin nervously, wondering what Mary would say when she received two hundred and twenty dollars. The thought flashed through his mind that he might intimate that they had doubled Joe's salary.

'Well, that's fine,' said Armadillo. 'I'll buy a drink.'

'Thanks, Armadillo, but I ain't got time right now. Mebby a little later, eh?'

'Aw, sure. See yuh later, Pete.'

Armadillo bowlegged his way across the street. Hank Ludden was crossing the street farther up, and they met in front of the War Paint Saloon, where they entered together.

'Snake's delight!' snorted the sheriff. 'I better think up a good lie to tell Mary, and I can't think a-tall.'

He walked back past the bank and headed for the other end of the town, intending to have a talk with Mary. A tall, thin man came from inside a hallway, and the sheriff recognized him as being the county treasurer, a slow-spoken, clerical sort of person.

'Hallo, Sheriff; I was hoping to see you.'

The treasurer of Arapaho County hitched up his trousers, drew out a handkerchief, and blew his nose violently.

'Wanted to see me?' Thus the sheriff indifferently. He did not care a great deal about the treasurer.

'Yes. The—er—treasurer's office has agreed to—er—do something which is probably irregular, and we will need you to sort of pave the way, as it were.

'Henry Ludden handed us his cheque for fifteen hundred dollars to-day, from which we are to pay Mary Lane the salary received by her lamented husband. It is supposed to be paid by the county, otherwise the said Mary Lane might not agree to accept it. And in order that she may understand it, I want you to intimate that the county is going to pay Joe Lane's salary to her for his unexpired term. Do I make myself plain?'

Pete Darcey yanked his hat down over one eye, while his five-fingered right hand dug deeply into the back of his head, his eyes half-closed, his mouth open.

'We felt sorry for the old man,' explained the treasurer. 'It is irregular, of course, but—you'll know what to say to her, Sheriff. You don't mind, do you?'

'Hell, no!' The sheriff leaned against the side of the building and watched the treasurer go briskly down the sidewalk.

'Three of a kind and a joker,' he wailed. 'I s'pose I might as well be good and damned for a three-hundred-and-thirty lie as to be an ordinary liar for a third of it.'

\*       \*       \*

It was suppertime when Hashknife and

Sleepy rode in at the little town of McCallville, if it might be designated a town. It was what might be termed a half-street town, as the three buildings were all on the same side of the road—the McCallville Hotel, part of the lower floor being the general store and post office, the McCallville Saloon, and the McCallville Restaurant.

About two hundred yards away from the town was the depot, a little boxlike affair, and farther to the north was a big loading corral. McCallville was not an interesting place. From the lack of paint, repairs, and general activity, it was plain to see that the population was not progressive or public-spirited.

The two cowboys rode out to the depot, tied their horses to a telegraph post, and sauntered around to the door. The depot agent, a cadaverous-looking, weary-eyed man, was asleep in his chair, an open pocketknife in one hand, a piece of pine board in the other. He had whittled himself to sleep.

The sound of their boot-heels awoke him, and he squinted sleepily. Hashknife leaned through the ticket-window and grinned widely.

'Hyah was?' said Hashknife.

'Awright. Whatcha want? Ticket?'

'No-o-o. Just drifted in to see if yuh know anybody that's goin' to ship some cows soon. We're lookin' for a free ride.'

'Shippin' cows!' The agent spat disgustedly. 'There ain't been a cow shipped from here since it became fashionable for 'em to wear horns.'

'Thasso? Pshaw, I heard that lots o' cows was shipped from McCallville.'

'Was, but ain't no more. Not for a year or so. Somebody sure lied heavily to yuh, friend. If any cows was shipped from here, I'd sure know about it. I'm high, low, jack, and the game around this misnamed shippin' point.'

'Yeah, I reckon yuh would,' admitted Hashknife. 'We've been lied to, it seems.'

Hashknife thanked him for the information and they rode down to the loading corral. To all appearances the corral had not been used for a long time. The hinges of the gates were rusty and the loading platform, a movable piece of planking which was used to connect the loading chute with the cars, had been lying in the weeds for months.

'If Scotty McLeod and his friend stole

133

HL cattle, they sure didn't ship 'em from here,' declared Sleepy.

Hashknife shook his head and climbed back on his horse. It was growing dark, and they went back to the hotel, where they ate supper. Only two other men entered the hotel, and from their conversation it was easy to see that they were in business.

After supper they went to the McCallville Saloon, where they bought some cigars, only to throw them away later on, and talked with the bartender. To him Hashknife told the same tale he had told to the depot agent.

'Ain't been shippin' nothin' from here,' replied the bartender. 'Town is on the bum. You fellers ought to go up to Casco. They ship once in a while, and yuh might get a chance to travel with 'em.'

'Didja ever meet a feller named Scotty McLeod?' asked Hashknife.

The bartender took this under advisement.

'Nope. I knowed a feller by that name in Iowa. He died before I left. It must be a different McLeod.'

'Prob'ly is,' said Hashknife seriously. 'This one has red hair.'

'It's a different one, then. Mine had

white. He was eighty years old. What are yuh goin' to have?'

They named their choice. Another man, one of the diners, came in and joined them at the bar. He was the proprietor of the general merchandise store and was not averse to accepting a drink.

For possibly half an hour they stood at the bar, talking about McCallville, which, according to the storekeeper, was on its last legs. Some horsemen went past, bridle chains jingling, the horses going slowly.

The bartender walked to the window, drew aside the curtain, and looked out.

'Who was it?' asked the merchant as the bartender came back.

'I didn't get a look at 'em. Don't think they stopped.'

'Ain't much travel through here, eh?' queried Hashknife.

'Not much,' replied the merchant. 'I'll buy now.'

'You want the same, gents?' asked the bartender.

Sleepy shook his head quickly.

'I don't like to be particular, but I don't like that kind of liquor.'

'This kind?'

The bartender picked up the bottle

rather indignantly and shook it viciously.

'Yeah, that's it.'

'Sa-a-ay, don'tcha know good liquor when yuh taste it? That's twenty years old, pardner. Ol' Crow, by golly!'

'Thasso?' Sleepy's eyes opened wide. 'That accounts for the feathers I've got in my mouth. They ort to pick their crows before they bottle 'em.'

'There ain't no feathers in this stuff, y'betcha. Look at it.'

He handed the bottle to Sleepy, who squinted through it at the light.

'Jist as clear as a—'

Crash!

The bottle exploded into a thousand pieces, spraying them all with broken glass and liquor, while from out in the street came the report of a gun. The heavy glass bottle deflected the bullet into the back-bar, where it smashed a few more bottles and splintered a corner of the mirror.

For a second they were all paralyzed. The next second they were all on the floor. Hashknife flung himself backward towards a card-table, where he landed sitting down with a gun in his hand.

Steadying himself on his left hand he proceeded to shoot out the hanging lamp over the bar, plunging the saloon into darkness. There was only a few seconds' space between the smashing of the bottle and the putting out of the lamp.

'He-e-e-ey! Quit shootin', you damn' fool!' yelped the bartender.

He probably thought both shots had been fired from outside. Hashknife squinted towards the street, across which he could see only the skyline of the hills.

'Shot at me,' he decided. 'Mebbe the window glass deflected it a little. Bullet goes past neck and busts up that bottle.' Then aloud—

'Sleepy!'

'Present,' grunted Sleepy. 'I'm settin' on the merchant. How are yuh, bartender?'

'Down low,' replied the bartender. 'And I'm goin' to stay low, too. I've got a sawed-off shotgun in my hands, and I'm sure goin' to be generous with buckshot if anybody fools around me.'

'Somebody must 'a' had it in for you,' observed Hashknife.

'Me?' The bartender snorted indignantly. 'Who in hell do yuh reckon wanted to kill me?'

'You prob'ly gave somebody a drink of yore Old Crow,' snickered Sleepy. 'Feller can't be too careful in this day and age.'

'Mebbe it's funny to you, but it sure ain't to me.'

'Nor to me.' Thus the merchant. 'Some of that glass cut me in the face. Can't we light a lamp?'

'After I get out,' said Hashknife quickly.

'No lamp,' declared the bartender. 'I don't suppose there will be another lamp lit in this place to-night. To-morrow I'm goin' away and I ain't comin' back.'

'Think you'll go back to Iowa?' asked Sleepy.

'Some're back there. Say, why don'tcha go out and see if that assassin is still there?'

'C'mere and give me yore riot gun,' said Sleepy.

'Yea-a-ah? If I wanted a riot gun very bad, I'd sure have ambition enough to go and git one. I may have to come out some time, but that ain't right now, pardner.'

*     *     *

Hashknife slid back against the wall, walked to the front of the room, and peered out through the broken window. The light was good enough for him to see that there was no one in the street in the immediate

138

vicinity of the saloon.

'I reckon the storm is over,' he told them. 'Nobody in the street.'

He walked outside and looked around. Several people were standing in front of the hotel, and now they came down towards the saloon, questioning Hashknife. Sleepy and the merchant came out, and Hashknife left it to the merchant to explain what had happened.

The men from the hotel were unable to throw any light on the situation. Hearing the voices, the bartender came out, still carrying his riot gun. He locked the door behind him and announced that the McCallville Saloon was closed for repairs.

'Was they shootin' at you?' asked one of the men.

'Yuh danged right!' The bartender was emphatic. 'If one of these men hadn't shoved a bottle of hooch between me and that gun, I'd be a lily-holder right now.'

'I had a hunch to do it,' said Sleepy seriously.

'We're bunched up too much,' said one of the men, turning back towards the hotel. 'I'd hate to be mistaken for the bartender.'

'That's the way I feel,' laughed Hashknife.

He started towards the hitch-rack, and Sleepy followed him, while the rest of the men headed towards the hotel.

They mounted, then rode north until they were out of sight of the street, when they swung east again, going slowly, riding knee to knee.

'That was close, Sleepy,' said Hashknife softly. 'It missed my neck by an inch. I was leanin' forward.'

'That's right. You was at my left, and the bullet came from yore left and behind yuh. What's the answer, Hashknife?'

'The man who wrote me that letter, Sleepy. The same man who wrote the instructions to Scotty McLeod.'

'The dirty bushwhacker!'

'Sh-h-h! He prob'ly knows he missed, and he's out here somewhere waitin' for another chance.'

'What's our next move?'

'Go through Crow Rock Canyon in the dark, cowboy.'

'Holy cats! Suppose he lays for us in there? We ain't got a ghost of a chance in there, Hashknife.'

'We have at night. In the daylight he could pick us off. If he works close he can't be sure. We'll just have to ride with a gun

140

in our hand. It'll be as dark as the inside of a stovepipe for two miles.'

'And expectin' every minute to get a shot in the dark.'

'Mebbe. Anyway, I've got a scheme that might help us. It sure is lucky we've got a pair of broncs we can depend on.'

There was no moon. They had ridden in over a sort of trail from the east end of Crow Rock Canyon, but they did not know where that trail was now. Ahead of them, sharply etched against the horizon, was the U-shaped cleft in the mountains, where nature had cut a canal-like canyon completely through the range of mountains.

There was little variance in altitude in the floor of the narrow canyon, which was principally of solid rock, although here and there a slide had filled in enough soil to start a growth of jack pines.

In places it was barely wide enough for a single rider to pass between the rocky sides, and again it would attain a width of fifty feet or more. Nature had provided a pass through the Twisted River Mountains and then proceeded to fill it with snow in the winter and slides in the spring, which precluded any chance of its ever being a popular pass.

They reached the mouth of the canyon and stopped to give the horses a breathing spell. The last half-mile had been a heavy grade, over rocks and through thickets. Behind them the hills sloped sharply towards McCallville, but the valley was only a black bowl, unlighted by the few faint stars. Ahead of them were the steep rocky slopes where the breeze whispered through the pines, and the inklike blot of Crow Rock Canyon.

Hashknife dismounted and tied his reins loosely to his saddle-horn.

'We're goin' to herd 'em through, Sleepy,' he said softly. 'Tie up yore reins. In that canyon the Devil himself couldn't tell whether a horse carried a rider or not. We may lose a horse, but that's better than losin' a life.'

'It sure is.' Sleepy dismounted and fixed his reins. 'Two miles ain't far to walk. Shall we pack our rifles?'

'Nope. A six-gun is enough, Sleepy. All set?'

They led their horses to the mouth of the narrow canyon, where Hashknife put his horse in the lead and clucked to him sharply. A moment later the mouth of the canyon was empty, and only the slither of hoof and boot came from the inky depths to show that men and beasts were passing through.

There was no possibility of fast travelling. The lead horse picked its way slowly around the rocky turns, while Hashknife and Sleepy travelled within reach of the second horse.

They were unable to see anything. In that deep cleft even the faint starlight was cut off. It was like travelling through the bore of a great tunnel. There was no conversation except an occasional grunt when one of them came in sharp contact with a corner at one of the right-angle turns.

They were possibly a third of the way through the canyon when Sleepy's horse stopped short and both men bumped into it. A quick investigation showed that Hashknife's horse had also stopped.

For possibly ten seconds neither man moved. It was plainly evident that there was something ahead of the horses. Touching Sleepy on the arm, indicating for him to stay where he was, Hashknife worked his way slowly past the animals, whispering softly to them. At the head of his horse he stopped and tried to penetrate the darkness, listening closely. But there was only the soft murmur of the breeze from high up on the cliffs.

Then he moved slowly ahead, one arm outstretched. Suddenly his hand came in contact with a wire which had been stretched across the narrow canyon, and before he realized what he was doing he pulled sharply on it.

From just ahead and to the right came the flash and report of a gun. Hashknife ducked low, jerking at his gun, while from around the horses came the slither of Sleepy's boots on the rocks as he shoved past the startled beasts. 'Hashknife!' he called sharply.

'All right, pardner,' replied Hashknife. Sleepy came in beside him.

'Did you fire that shot?' he asked.

'Nope.' Hashknife chuckled softly and guided Sleepy's hand to the wire. 'Feel that.'

'For gosh' sake! Barb' wire, eh? They came through ahead of us,' whispered Sleepy. 'Where did that shot come from?'

'I'll tell you in a minute.' Hashknife worked his way along the wire and found where it circled a small jack pine. He ducked under the wire and followed it a few feet, where it ended at a piece of the broken ledge.

Working his fingers down in the ledge he managed to dislodge a short revolver, around the trigger of which had been looped a single strand of wire. He came back along the wire to Sleepy and squatted down on his heels while he explained about the set-gun.

'I happened to be lookin' towards it and seen the flash go up. Bushwhackers don't usually shoot in the air, Sleepy.'

'All right, cowboy. But what does it mean?'

'It was meant to stop us. They felt sure our horses would stop at the wire. We'd get off and run into it, shootin' off the gun. *Sabe?* And that would stop us from goin' ahead, 'cause we'd feel sure that a reception was bein' planned for us. They want us to be in this canyon at daybreak.'

'Which would give them a sweet chance to pick us off from the sides, eh? Let's go.'

It did not take long to remove the wire, and they started on, hardly knowing what to expect now. But nothing impeded their progress. After what seemed an interminable length of time they came out

145

of the canyon, mounted quickly, and rode down the slopes towards Arapaho City.

It was still too dark for any danger of ambush, so they travelled south-west past McLeod's cabin, and struck his road to town.

Arapaho City was in darkness. They stabled their horses and went to their room at the hotel, where Hashknife produced the revolver which he had taken from the rock crevice, and they examined it.

It was of a cheap make, brightly nickelled, and of thirty-eight calibre. Only one cartridge had been placed in it. And on the bottom of the butt, evidently engraved with great care, were the initials S. McL.

'Scotty McLeod's gun, eh?' mused Hashknife, as he lighted a cigarette over the chimney of the lamp.

'Blamed fool to put his initials on a gun!' snorted Sleepy.

'But he didn't set it,' grinned Hashknife. 'The man who set it didn't expect us to take it along. We'll talk with McLeod in the mornin'.'

'But what I don't see is this: What good did it do us to go to McCallville, Hashknife?'

'Well, we met some nice people, got shot

146

at, collected a nice, shiny gun, and got home safe. What more would yuh want in one evenin'? I feel that we've been entertained, Sleepy.'

'That's all right. I appreciate their efforts and all that, but what do we gain by it? There wasn't any chance of McLeod takin' cows through Crow Rock Canyon to-night. I don't believe there has been any cows through there. Wasn't any sign of cows through there.

'If you went to McCallville to get shot at, yuh sure got yore wish. An inch more to the left, and you'd be of no further use to me. But I don't see what good it done yuh.'

Hashknife grinned slowly as he drew off his boots.

'I just wanted to find out if they was waitin' for Scotty McLeod or for me.'

'Do yuh know now?'

'Well,' grinned Hashknife, 'of course, there's always a chance that they were shootin' at the bartender. But the bartender never had any idea of comin' through Crow Rock Canyon to-night.'

'He's prob'ly half-way to Iowa by this time,' laughed Sleepy. 'He'll brag about that all the rest of his life, and I'll bet he'll tell it so many times that after a while it'll be one of the biggest killin's ever pulled off in the West.'

'Prob'ly wear his hair long and call himself "Two-Gun Ike" or somethin' like that,' grinned Hashknife. He had taken off his boots and was examining a blister which he had contracted in his two-mile walk. Sleepy rolled into bed with a sigh of relief.

'It's a wonder to me that they didn't do somethin' to our horses,' said Sleepy. 'They were the only two at the hitch-rack in McCallville.'

Hashknife shook his head quickly.

'It looks as if they saw a possible chance to kill or cripple one of us there in the saloon. And if they failed to do this, the fact that they shot at us in there might cause us to wait until daylight. What they wanted us to do was to ride through that canyon in daylight.'

'Yuh mean they wanted to pot-shoot us in that narrow pass?' asked Sleepy.

Hashknife nodded quickly. 'It looks like it to me. I'm just wonderin' if they wasn't playin' a cinch game.'

He got off the bed and walked to the corner of the room where they had left their rifles.

He examined one of them closely,

opening and closing the action, investigating with his finger. Then he took the other one and gave it the same inspection. Then he stood it against the wall, walked back to the table, blew out the lamp, and rolled into bed.

'It's a good thing we didn't do battle with 'em, Sleepy,' he said seriously. 'They plumb ruined the firin'-pins on both of them rifles.'

'The hell they did! Can yuh beat that?'

'I'm goin' to try and do it, Sleepy.'

'Uh-huh. Say! Were them pins all right when we got the guns from the sheriff?' The idea was so good that Sleepy sat up in bed.

'That's a question I've been askin' myself.'

'Oh, hell!' Sleepy subsided heavily. 'I'm always late. By golly, I'll bet that when Gabriel blows his horn and says, "Sleepy Stevens, come forth," I'll come fifth.'

'I'm glad you thought of it, anyway, Sleepy.'

'Oh, so am I. I gave you a chance to swipe my thunder.'

'Good-night, Sleepy.'

'I thought of that quite a while ago myself. Good-night.'

## CHAPTER NINE

# HASHKNIFE MAKES A VISIT

The following morning Amos Hardy, cattle-buyer, arrived in Arapaho City on his semi-annual buying trip. Amos was short, fat, with a big, smiling face, a typical good-natured fat man, but with an uncanny judgment concerning the weight and worth of cattle.

He wended his way to the Arapaho Hotel, where he ate his breakfast, after which he went to the War Paint Saloon to renew old acquaintances. Amos was a mixer, a hail fellow well met. He shook hands with the bartender, bought a handful of very bad cigars, and listened to the news of the Twisted River Range.

'Joe Lane dead, eh? Lucky Joe. Hm-m-m. Gosh, that's too bad. I didn't know this Naylor. McLeod, I didn't know either. And Hank Ludden killed Joe Lane, eh? That's bad. How's Joe's widder? All right? Pretty girl. She won't be a widder long.

'Is Hank Ludden still runnin' the Hard Luck Ranch? He is? Stick there in spite of it all, eh? Huh! Well'—Hardy shifted his cigar and puffed thoughtfully—'this kinda looks as though the hard-luck still sticks to the HL. Have you seen old Dutch O'Day lately?'

'He was in the other day. We don't see much of him.'

'Mean as ever, I suppose. I never was out to see him but once. My, my! Boy, he's got the worst tongue I ever heard. He cursed me in and he cursed me out. I wouldn't go out to see him if he'd give me a trainload of cows.'

And so Amos rambled on, getting a few drinks under his wide belt and acquiring plenty of local knowledge which would be food for conversation later on.

He was beginning to shorten his drinks when Corliss rode in from the Five Box and came to the War Paint.

'H'lo, Corliss,' greeted Amos. 'How's the cow business?'

Corliss laughed and shook hands with him.

'O'Day was sayin' yesterday that it was about time for you to be showin' up, Hardy. How are yuh, anyway?'

'I'm jus' right, old-timer. Have a drink. I'll bet that ain't all that O'Day said about me.'

Corliss laughed and shook his head.

'I reckon he don't like you, Hardy. But don't let that bother yuh.'

'Nothin' bothers me,' expansively. 'As long as he'll sell me good beef he can cuss me and be darned to him. Well, here's to the pit of your stomach and may it never rust out.'

And while Amos and the foreman of the Five Box drank to each other—including, of course, the bartender, who bought every third time—Hashknife and Sleepy had breakfast at the Pekin Café, after which they took their rifles to the sheriff's office.

The sheriff was anxious to hear what they found at Crow Rock Canyon, and Hashknife told it to him in detail, showing him the revolver which carried McLeod's initials. Then he opened the rifles and pointed out the disabled firing-pins. It had only taken a few moments work with a screwdriver to put both rifles out of commission.

'Uh-huh.' The sheriff nodded thoughtfully. 'Hartley, yo're not buckin' ignorance in this. They're not overlookin' anything.'

'Except that we're still alive,' added

Hashknife.

'Yeah, that's true. Let's go back and have a little talk with Scotty. He's eatin' breakfast.'

Scotty greeted them with a smile and came up to the bar, carrying his cup of coffee.

'Very well, considerin' my position in the matter.'

'I was just wonderin' if you owned a six-shooter, McLeod.'

'A six-shooter? No, ye wouldn't call it that. I've a five-shooter.'

'Nickel-plated thirty-eight, with yore initials on the butt?'

Scotty nodded quickly, squinting at Hashknife.

'Ye've been in my tr-runk, it seems.'

Hashknife laughed softly.

'You hadn't ought to put yore name on a gun. It might cause yuh trouble.'

'That gun shouldn't cause any one trouble. Ye couldn't hit the wall of a house at ten paces with it.'

'I reckon that's true,' grinned Hashknife. 'I found it in Crow Rock Canyon yesterday.'

'Ye did? My gun?' Scotty shook his head. 'I've never been in Crow Rock

Canyon in me life and I've never carried that gun anywhere. It wasn't worth carryin'.'

'Yuh never was in Crow Rock Canyon, eh? Never went through to McCallville?'

'Never.' Scotty shook his head. 'I've never been in McCallville in me life and I've had no occasion to go to Crow Rock Canyon, although I know where it is. If ye're not jokin' with me, someone must have searched through me trunk and took the gun. I'm sure it was there just before I was arrested.'

'I guess they did,' agreed Hashknife.

Back in the office the sheriff shook his head.

'I'm thinkin' that Scotty is an awful liar. I haven't mentioned that note to him, and he'll probably lie when I do.'

'Probably,' agreed Hashknife. 'We'll just have to wait and see what happens next.'

They left the office and wandered to the War Paint Saloon, where they ran into Amos Hardy and Corliss. Hashknife would have given much to know that Hardy was in town so that he might have avoided him, but it was too late now.

Hardy was expansively drunk, and he yelped with delight when he caught a glimpse of Hashknife and Sleepy.

'Hell's hinges!' he yelped, shoving away from the bar, his fat face wreathed in a smile, his legs a bit uncertain. 'Hashknife, you old bed slat! Welcome to our reception! Sleepy, you old hedgehog! Ha, ha, ha, ha, ha! Shake Uncle Amos's paw and say yuh feel pleased to meet him. Greeting and salutations.'

He wheezed and pawed at them, stepping on Sleepy's toes in his exuberance of joy.

'Keep yore feet down!' growled Sleepy. 'Ain't the rest of the world wide enough for yuh without walkin' on me?'

'Ha, ha, ha, ha, ha!' Amos guffawed widely and tacked back to the bar, waving both hands at Hashknife and Sleepy.

'C'mon and get it. Ha, ha, ha, ha! By golly, it sure is fine to meet a friend. Yessir, it sure—'

He squinted at Corliss, shut one eye tight, and turned his head to look at Hashknife.

'Misser Corliss,' he said solemnly, 'I want you to meet Misser Hartley and Misser Stevens. Gen'lmen, thish is Misser Corliss. He's foreman of the Five Box.'

Hashknife shook hands with Corliss, a
155

half-grin on his lips, and Corliss laughed.

'Smith brothers, eh?' he chuckled.

'Smith brothers?' Amos squited at Corliss.

He was not so drunk that all reason had fled.

'He-e-ey!' he snorted. 'What have I done now?'

'Killed the Smith brothers,' laughed Hashknife.

'Oh!' Amos goggled drunkenly. 'Is it all right?'

'Sure.' They stood at the bar and had their drinks.

'That Smith idea was sort of an inspiration,' laughed Hashknife.

'A man has a right to a name,' said Corliss. 'Let's have another.'

One more was just one too many for Amos, and Corliss took him across the street to the hotel, where he registered for him and put him to bed.

'I sure hope the deaths of the Smith brothers won't cause a fallin' off in the Hartley and Stevens families,' said Sleepy as they sat down in the shade of the saloon porch.

'It won't hurt none, Sleepy. The men who were lookin' for us already knew us, so the rest of the bunch don't matter. I'd like to know who Amos talked to about us after he spoke to Hank Ludden about writin' that letter to me.'

'Probably won't remember.'

Corliss came back from the hotel and joined them.

'I tucked Amos in his little bed,' he grinned. 'Meetin' him almost made me forget what O'Day told me. He said if I met you fellows to tell yuh to come out and see him.'

'What's the idea?' asked Hashknife.

'I'll be darned if I know, Hartley. Of course, you haven't known O'Day very long and you wouldn't see any change in him, but something' has gone wrong with the man.

'I've kept my job because I was able to stand for his disposition. For years, ever since he got hurt, he's been the meanest old devil on earth. Nothin' suited him. He'd cuss yuh for doin' wrong and he'd cuss yuh for doin' right.

'There was only one satisfaction, and that was the fact that we could get away from him. He cursed everybody, everythin'. Even subscribed for several newspapers so he could get somethin' to curse about.

'Sent East for one of them air-rifles so he could shoot the dogs. Shoot a horse just to see it jump, and then laugh about it. He wanted to hurt somethin'! No one ever came to see him the second time.

'But now'—Corliss shook his head slowly—'I dunno what's the matter with him. He don't swear any more. Not even at How Long, the Chink. Asked us to come up to the ranch-house and play poker with him. Honey Moon won forty dollars from him last night, and O'Day never even swore about it.

'Honey thinks the old man is goin' to die. I tell yuh it's pretty noticeable when How Long sees it. He don't *sabe*. I asks him what he thinks and he say:

'"No *sabe*. Long time, nobody good. Plenty mad. How Long cook bad, dlive bad ... Chinaman not worth kill. Swear plenty from evelything. Now, How Long velly good cook, dlive nice. No swear at How Long. Say 'please.' Yo *sabe?* How Long velly good Chinaman. Like fine."

'And that's how the Chink feels about it, Hartley.'

Hashknife grinned.

'Mebby he got tired of bein' bad.'

Corliss grunted shortly. 'Mebbe.'

'I'd just as soon ride out and see him,' said Hashknife. 'It sure must be a novelty to have O'Day ask yuh out there.'

'Novelty, hell! It's a shock. If yuh want to go out right away, I'll be ready as soon as I get the mail.'

Hashknife and Sleepy got their horses and rode away with Corliss. He seemed a different man than he was the day they had met him at Scotty McLeod's place after the killing of Naylor. Except for the broken nose, Corliss would have been a good-looking man. The muscles of his big torso rippled beneath the thin shirt, and he held his body straight in the saddle.

The talk drifted to Scotty McLeod's troubles as they passed the old road which led to McLeod's little shack. 'I dunno what you fellers thought of us that day,' said Corliss. 'It kinda looked as though we had started somethin' we couldn't finish, didn't it? You know how cowmen feel about sheep—even a few sheep. It was like a slap in the face.

'I'll admit that I was a little sudden,' Corliss laughed. 'It was worth it to see the expression of that nester's face when he seen the sheep on the end of my rope. I made him walk to the gate with me. I figured I could get out of sight before he could get back to the house and grab his rifle, but I was all wrong.

'He went back there like a scared rabbit goin' to a hole, and it was only about ten seconds until he was throwin' lead. And he's a good shot. Moon and Naylor were farther back on the hill. They thought everythin' was all right.'

'About how far did he have to shoot at Naylor?' asked Hashknife.

'I dunno. Must 'a' been between two hundred and two hundred and fifty yards— mebbe more.'

Hashknife nodded. He had estimated it at about that distance.

'I have heard that Joe Lane was very friendly with McLeod.'

'I dunno much about that,' said Corliss. 'Joe Lane was all right. Bein' a deputy sheriff kinda swelled his head, but outside of that he was all right, I reckon.'

'Did you ever suspect Joe Lane of rustlin'?'

Corliss shook his head quickly.

'No. I don't suppose anybody else ever did, Hartley. There's nothin' now, except Hank Ludden's word for it. But I don't think Hank would lie about it. Joe was his son-in-law.'

'And there were two other men, Corliss. Ludden says there were three in the bunch.'

'That's what he says, and he's prob'ly right. Who they are and where they went is a question. There are a lot of riders in the Twisted River Range, Hartley. There's six outfits between here and Casco. On the other side of the range are several more outfits within a day's ride of here. Pickin' out two men from that bunch would be quite a job.'

They rode in at the Five Box Ranch and tied their horses at a corral fence. The Five Box ranch-house was a one-story, rambling sort of place, with a wide veranda around the front and one side. Behind the house was a big stable and to the left of this was a series of corrals. The bunk-house was a long log building, about a hundred feet away from the ranch-house, and was the only log building in the group. It was evidently at one time the ranch-house building, as all the rest of the group were of frame construction and paint had been used lavishly. The house was blue and the stable was red.

'Yuh ought to paint the bunk-house white and change the brand to US,' suggested Hashknife as they dismounted.

'Might be a good idea,' laughed Corliss. 'O'Day hates red and blue, so he used them colours. It gave him an excuse to curse the ranch along with everythin' else.'

They followed Corliss up to the ranch-house veranda, where they found O'Day, snuggled down in an easy-chair, watching How Long, who was trying to plant a rose-bush in the front yard.

★    ★    ★

O'Day greeted them with a smile, although he did not offer to shake hands with them. He looked even smaller, humped down in that big chair. Perhaps it was because he was not wearing a hat, and his thin, colourless hair was sticking up on his head like some foxtail grass.

'Sure, I'm havin' the devil's own time,' he told them. 'Did ye ever have to do any gardenin' by Chinese proxy? Ah, it's a task. How Long is a fine Chinaman, but he has an oriental idea of doin' things. Sure, he came near plantin' my rose-bush upside down.'

162

Hashknife laughed and sat down on the veranda, bracing his back against a post, while Sleepy sat down on the steps.

'Goin' to have a rose garden, eh?' asked Hashknife.

'Aye.' O'Day squinted against the sun, and the heavy lines of his thin face seemed to deepen. 'Dutch O'Day and a rose garden. Well, I've looked at thistles long enough, and it's time I was lookin' at the rose.'

'That's the right idea,' said Hashknife seriously.

O'Day nodded slowly, squinting at the Chinaman, who stood out in the yard, shovel in hand, waiting for his orders.

'If ye put yer feet in the hole, ye'd take root, How Long,' laughed O'Day. 'Put the root of the bush in the hole and fill in the dirt. But before ye do that, go and get some fertilizer.'

The Chinaman looked blankly at O'Day, who turned to Corliss.

'Will ye go wid him? By the time I've explained what fertilizer is, the bush will have died.'

Corliss laughed and motioned to the Chinaman, who followed him. O'Day watched them go and turned back to

Hashknife.

'Smith,' he said slowly, 'I want to thank ye for sayin' what ye did to me the other day. It made me so damn' mad that I got to thinkin'.'

'I'm glad yuh thought,' said Hashknife. 'But our names are not Smith. My name is Hartley and my pardner's name is Stevens. The Smith part of it was only a joke.'

O'Day squinted closely at Hashknife.

'Hartley? Now where did I hear—what do they call ye?'

'They usually call me Hashknife.'

'Aye! Hashknife Hartley. I've heard the name, and I've also heard of things ye have done, lad, ye and yer pardner. Well, well! No wonder ye wasn't afraid to throw me reputation into me teeth. Smith brothers!'

O'Day laughed softly and shook his head.

Honey Moon came clattering up the side steps and along the veranda, while around the corner came Corliss and the Chinaman, carrying fertilizer for the roses. O'Day called to Corliss, who came up to them.

'I want you two boys to meet Hashknife Hartley and his partner, Stevens,' said O'Day, chuckling softly. 'They're not the Smith brothers.'

'I knew that before we left town,' laughed Corliss.

'Oh, ye did, did ye?' grunted O'Day. 'Well, Moon didn't.'

'I shore didn't,' laughed Moon. 'I dunno what it's all about, but I s'pose it's all right.'

'Ye don't? Honey, I'm surprised at ye. Didn't ye ever hear of Hashknife Hartley?'

'Well, I may be ignorant,' laughed Moon, 'but I don't—'

'Do you?' O'Day spoke to Corliss, who shook his head.

'All I know is that Amos Hardy called 'em by those names. He came in on the mornin' train and got dead drunk.'

'Aye, it's about time for him to come through. Mebbe I better let him sober up and tell yuh who Hartley is, because he travels all through the cow country, and he's likely heard a lot more than I have.'

'I don't reckon there's anythin' worth tellin',' said Hashknife. 'Hardy would prob'ly lie a lot about us.'

'I've heard,' said O'Day seriously, 'that most of the lies they tell about you are the truth.'

'Suppose you tell us,' suggested Corliss.

'I'm the biggest liar of them all,' laughed

Hashknife. 'We're just a pair of ramblin punchers, that's all. A feller in Calumet called us a pair of tumbleweeds, and that covers us.'

'Do they lie about what ye done in the Thunder River country and up north of Wind River and the jobs here and there for the last few years? What about the Mission River gang? Do they lie about that? I could name ye a few names if ye wish.'

'Don't do it, O'Day,' smiled Hashknife. 'I do not know how it has been told to yuh, so I can't tell whether it's true or not. But me and Sleepy never talk about ourselves. He don't think I amount to much, and I know damn' well he don't. So there yuh are.

'If we've made reputations for ourselves, it wasn't because we went seekin' 'em. That part of it was the last thing on our minds. It hasn't paid us in money. Sometimes we have a hard job to get money enough to buy a fresh horse.'

'Ye mean that ye don't get paid for what ye do?'

'We don't hire out,' smiled Hashknife. 'There's no agreement between us and the rest of the world.'

'That's damn' poor business,' said

166

Honey Moon.

'We're not in business.'

'I wouldn't take a chance on bein' killed unless I was bein' well paid, y'betcha.'

'Wouldn't yuh?' smiled Hashknife. 'Do yuh ask for a raise in salary every time yuh top a bucker? Do yuh demand more money to chase a cow down the side of a canyon than yuh do for drivin' one along a flat piece of road?'

'That's different.'

'The principle is different, but the result is the same. It don't make much difference whether yuh die from a bullet or a broken neck.'

'All the same, I'll take a chance on my horse keepin' it's feet,' said Moon.

'And we take a chance on a rustler or murderer bein' a bad shot or a slow one.'

'That idea is all right,' smiled Corliss, 'but some day you'll meet one that shoots straight and shoots quick.'

'Then I'll be a memory,' grinned Hashknife.

*　　　*　　　*

The Chinaman had finished planting the bush. O'Day thanked him kindly, and the big How Long went away, grinning widely.

'I'm goin' to get more roses,' said O'Day. 'I'll borrow some of me hard-workin' punchers and attach 'em to the wood end of some shovels. Then I can set here and look out at roses and smell 'em. That's all there is left in life for me—just to set down and look on.'

'Why don't yuh get some artificial legs?' asked Hashknife. 'Yore knees are still good.'

'Pegs, do ye mean?'

'Not pegs—legs. Yuh might never become a footracer, but yuh could walk all around. They're made with braces and some springs, and yuh wear shoes on the feet. Mebby yuh'd have to pack a cane, but what if yuh did?'

O'Day smiled grimly.

'I've never seen anythin' like it, but I believe ye, Hartley. Now, where could I buy 'em?'

'I don't just know. I'll tell yuh who could get 'em for yuh, and that's Amos Hardy. He goes East after his buyin' trip is over, and he'd sure do it.'

'Mebbe not for me.' O'Day was thinking of the only time Amos Hardy had been at the Five Box and they had quarrelled over

168

the price of hides.

'He'd do it for me,' declared Hashknife. 'I'll tell him as soon as we get back.'

'Thank ye, Hartley. But I'd like to have a talk wid Hardy meself. He knows the cattle business, and I'd like to talk over the situation wid him. Suppose'—O'Day turned to Corliss—'ye bring him out here? You or one of the other boys take the buckboard in to Arapaho and bring him back.

'We quarrelled a long time ago, and he's not been here since. Hardy's firm pays cash for everythin' they buy, and it saves time. He takes mostly everythin' we have for sale, and his prices are as good as anybody offers. Corliss, ye might tell him that I was wrong on the price of hides, and that I'm sorry for the things I called him.'

'All right,' nodded Corliss. 'I'll ask him to come. Mebbe he won't, O'Day. Hardy is kinda touchy yuh know.'

'Not knowin' him very well, I dunno how his feelin's are. But I think he'll come.'

Corliss and Moon went off the veranda and headed for the stable. Dayne had just ridden in and was unsaddling.

'What do ye think of the Five Box, Hartley?' asked O'Day.

'Comfortable sort of a place. I like this long porch and the one-story buildings. The cattle business is good now.'

'Aye, its all right when you're all right. I loved the feel of a good horse between me legs, the trail dust in me nostrils, the smell of the chuck wagon. I loved the sight of the cattle along the skyline of the ridges, the round up crews of dirty, sweatin' punchers, the song and the arguments. Aye, and I loved the fights.

'But I disliked the loadin' pens, Hartley, the long strings of cattle cars, the bawlin' cattle, rattlin' their horns agin' the side of the cars—big, helpless hulks, goin' away to die. Ah, I may be a fool, but I disliked it. The money I got for them gave me little enjoyment.

'Since I've been hurt I haven't even seen a cattle train. I've not seen a cow loaded since then. So many are taken at a time, and I only know that there's that many less Five Box cattle in the Twisted River hills.'

Hashknife smiled softly. It was the first time he had ever seen that kind of sentiment in a cattleman.

'The day of the big herds is passin',' said O'Day sadly. 'In a few years there'll be no big ranges left. Nesters will be raisin' fruit and vegetables where we raised cattle. Barb' wire is comin' in, Hartley. This country can be irrigated, and irrigation will break up the ranges.'

'That is true,' nodded Hashknife. 'But it will be quite a while yet. The world must have meat, and it takes the ranges to furnish it in big quantities. I've been curious to know just why yuh invented the Five Box brand.'

O'Day laughed and leaned back in his chair.

'I wanted somethin' that no cow thief could alter into some other brand. I'd defy anybody to take a runnin' iron and change it so that it would look like any other registered brand.'

'Well, you sure got it,' grinned Hashknife. 'It's visible enough.'

O'Day shifted himself to an easier position and lowered his voice.

'Hartley, what are you workin' on here?'

'Workin' on?' Hashknife looked up at O'Day. 'That's hard to say, old-timer.'

'I see. Ye're not workin' for Hank Ludden, are ye?'

'I'm workin' for the right side,' said Hashknife slowly. 'I'm not sure yet just who is in the right.'

'I don't think I understand ye,' said O'Day.

'That's about all I can tell yuh.'

'It's none of me business, of course. I'd like to hire the two of ye. I know I'm goin' to need a prod once in a while because I'm not cured. I'm tryin' to change me disposition, but it's a hard pull. It's easier to be mean than kind after ye've been mean for so long.'

'Thank yuh for the jobs,' said Hashknife. 'But we wouldn't be worth much to yuh, O'Day. We'd be leavin' soon. Yuh can't scratch an itchin' foot and look at the same scenery.'

Came the rattle of a buckboard, and Corliss drove past the corner of the veranda, stopping his team long enough to ask O'Day if there was anything he wanted in town. The team was a half-broken span of sorrels, threatening any moment to throw themselves, under the strong pull of the lines.

They shot away from the ranch, and the buckboard faded out of sight in a cloud of dust.

'Won't ye stay for supper?' asked O'Day, when Hashknife and Sleepy got to their feet.

'Not to-day, thanks,' said Hashknife. 'We'll come out again.'

'Make it soon, boys. Thank ye for comin', and if there's any help ye want, don't hesitate to ask for it. And thank ye for suggestin' the legs. I'd try anythin'. My God, after settin' in a chair as long as I have, I'd try wings if somebody would suggest 'em.'

# CHAPTER TEN

## AN ARREST

A couple of hours' sleep was sufficient for Amos Hardy, and he came back to the War Paint Saloon, where he met Armadillo Jones. After a drink to renew old acquaintances, Armadillo told him about Hashknife and Sleepy's being in Arapaho and that they were handling the troubles of the Hard Luck Ranch.

Amos dimly remembered introducing them to Corliss by their right names, and asked Armadillo if they were travelling incognito.

'You better have another drink,' said

173

Armadillo. 'Mebbe one more drink of War Paint's best will unravel yore words so a white man can *sabe* 'em.'

'I just wanted to know if they were usin' different names.'

'Oh, yeah; Smith.'

'Uh-huh!' grunted Amos. 'I reckon I made a *faux pas.*'

'A foo paw, eh? We'll pass that one and have the drink. You don't ache any place, do yuh, Amos?'

Amos shook his head slowly as he drank his liquor. Then he wiped his lips thoughtfully and said:

'I reckon I'm *de trop* with Hashknife.'

Armadillo dropped his glass on the bar, blinked violently, and headed for the door.

'Where yuh goin'?' asked Amos.

'I'm goin' to git me a book-tionary, and then I'm comin' back and worry you a while.'

Amos laughed and invited the bartender to become his bottle partner.

'I want everybody to be happy,' said Amos. 'You can't run out on me unless yuh shut up the shop. I never get drunk until I get to Arapaho City. It's so darned far away from the rest of the world that nobody knows what I do.'

'You buyin' cattle?' Thus the bartender.

'Y'betcha. I need five hundred head. Spot cash.'

'Lotta money. Got it with yuh?'

'I suppose yuh want to play single-handed stud, eh? Nope. Money's in the Arapaho Bank. Signed cheque is in my pocket. I draw what I need. That's how we get the pick of the beef.

'These old cowmen are funny. They want money, not cheques. My firm carries a balance in every bank where we do business. Oh, not a big balance, of course. But when I start out, I've got a hunch where I'll land the stuff, so they play the game with me and have the money all set. They've sure got confidence in little Amos.'

'You just about buy all the stuff around here, don'tcha?'

'Any place I go, I land the business. I'm too fat to be a crook. Honest Amos Hardy. It's took me all my life to win that name, and I wouldn't be crooked for less'n a million. Drink welcome, God knows you're hearty.'

Corliss came in as they were drinking, and Amos whooped with joy.

'It was a great Democrat victory, and I'm about to be inaugurated,' he told Corliss.

'This time I'll put you to bed.'

'That's a job,' said Corliss, who was a trifle proud of his ability to carry liquor. They had several drinks, and Corliss delivered the message from O'Day.

'Go out to see that old reptile?' wailed Amos. 'That old jug of profanity? Me? Sa-a-ay, feller! Huh! Have another and you'll see things different.'

Corliss did not urge him. He knew what had happened to Amos the one time he had been out there, and he did not blame him for not wanting to go back again. But the more liquor Amos drank the more indignant he became.

'Can yuh beat that?' he wailed. 'Asks me to come out there to see him. Don't he think I've got any feelin's? What does he think I am? I'm sprised at yuh, Corliss, for askin' me.'

Hashknife and Sleepy rode into Arapaho City and entered the War Paint during one of Amos's discourses. Amos whooped with joy and insisted on dragging them to the bar and telling all about Dutch O'Day's wanting to see him. Hashknife made no comment, but let Amos wail as loud as he wanted to.

The sheriff drifted in and joined the

crowd, of which Amos insisted on being toastmaster.

'I'm a nightingale,' he told them. 'I'm a whippoorwill and a nightingale, mixed with a strain of canary and medderlark. My voice sounds to me like the tinklin' of bells.'

'Cowbells,' said Sleepy. 'And as a birdologist, yo're all off the grade. Yore pedigree right now is one hundred per cent crow with a touch of buzzard. You've been eatin' bird-seed when yuh should have been dead a week.'

Sleepy was willing to admit that Amos Hardy was a good cattle-buyer, but he hated to hear even a drunken man brag about himself. But Amos did not care. Sleepy's sarcastic remark went in one ear and out the other.

'I know what I'm goin' to do,' declared Amos. 'I'm goin' out to see Dutch O'Day.'

'Yore crazy,' said the sheriff. 'You let O'Day alone.'

'Thasso?' Amos flared drunkenly. 'Crazy, eh? I'm just drunk enough to talk to that mummy-faced old chuckwalla. Las' time he told me a few things—thish time I'm gonna tell him a few. C'mon, Corliss.'

'You better stay here,' advised the

sheriff. And advice was something that Amos would not take—not in his condition.

'Don't tell me what to do!' snorted Amos. 'I'm free, white, and twenty-one. I've spent a lot of money with the darned old caterpillar, and I'm goin' to tell him all about his ancestors.

'I've got a list of every shipment I ever bought from him, every darned cow! And I'm goin' to show him how much money I've spent with him. By golly, he can't curse me and keep m' trade. C'mon, foreman of the Five Box.'

Corliss shook his head at the sheriff, but followed Amos outside and over to the buckboard, where Amos insisted on driving. But Corliss shoved him to the other side of the seat and took the reins himself.

As he turned the half-broken team away from the hitch-rack, Amos leaned forward, whipped off his hat, and struck one of the horses across the rump, which caused the team to whirl wildly and almost upset the buckboard.

'A nice feller when he's sober, but a damn' fool when he's drunk,' declared the sheriff as he and Hashknife started for the office, followed by Sleepy.

'He'll sober up before he gets back,' said Hashknife.

'He prob'ly will. Did yuh go out to see O'Day?'

'Yeah. Found him havin' roses planted in the front yard.'

'My God! Roses? Must have gone crazy. Say, I told McLeod about that note yuh found. He started to deny it, but shut up like a clam. Old Armadillo came down here a while ago. I was out, so he took it upon himself to go back and talk to McLeod. I suppose Armadillo thought it was all right. After he went away I told McLeod about that note.'

'Started to deny it?' queried Hashknife.

'Yeah. Then he shut up about it. Said he'd like to see the tall one of the Smith brothers.'

'Oh, he did, eh?' Hashknife surmised that Armadillo had told McLeod who the Smith brothers were, but he did not tell the sheriff.

'Mind if I talk with him alone?' asked Hashknife.

'N-o-o, I reckon not. Go ahead. If he tells yuh anythin', I know you'll tell me.'

'You think so, do yuh?' said Hashknife

to himself, but to the sheriff he merely nodded.

Sleepy and the sheriff sat down in the office, while Hashknife went back to McLeod's cell. McLeod had heard them come in, and was at the bars.

'You wanted to see me?' asked Hashknife.

'Yes. Armadillo Jones told me who you were, and that you were tryin' to find out who was stealin' from the Hard Luck Ranch.'

'Quite an order, don'tcha think, McLeod?'

'It has never been done. A while ago the sheriff accused me of bein' one of the thieves. Where did ye find that note?'

'In yore coat, hangin' on the wall of yore cabin.'

McLeod's amazement was genuine. He scratched his red hair violently and squinted at Hashknife. He felt that Hashknife was telling the truth, although he, McLeod, knew nothing about the note.

'That beats the record!'

'It does,' agreed Hashknife, grinning. 'But unless it can be explained, yo're up against it awful hard, McLeod.'

McLeod shook his head.

'But I can't explain it. Neither can I explain how ye happened to find me gun in Crow Rock Canyon. I've never been there, I tell ye. I'll admit in court that I shot at a man, but I'll insist that he got what was comin' to him, and I'll admit no rustlin'.'

'You were a good friend of Joe Lane?'

'Yes. I liked the lad. He often came out to see me.'

'He was killed for stealin' cattle.'

'That's tr-r-rue. But does that make me one? Man, there's a plot to make things awful har-r-rd for Scotty McLeod.'

He shook his head sadly, a dismal expression in his blue eyes.

'It's bad enough to be hung for killin' a man, but I've no likin' to be branded a thief into the bargain. The prosecutin' attorney was in to see me this mornin', and he asked me who my attorney might be. I've no attorney. What good would one be to me? All the ar-r-rguments in the world would only bring it back to the fact that I defended myself and killed a man.'

Hashknife laughed softly as he rolled a smoke.

'It sure looks bad for yuh, McLeod. I told Ludden I'd try and find out who was stealin' HL cattle. That's a big job. I've got a theory, tha'sall. I don't believe you was with Joe Lane. You say you was in town, and must have left here shortly before Lane was killed. I'm goin' to believe that, whether any one else believes it or not.'

'Are you goin' to try and prove that I'm not a thief?'

'I'm goin' to try it, McLeod. Everythin' is against me, but I'll do what I can. Don't say anythin' about it. Keep still about that note and the gun. *Sabe?*'

Hashknife went back to the sheriff and Sleepy, but told the sheriff that McLeod had nothing new to tell. While they were talking a man came in whom Hashknife recognized as being the prosecuting attorney.

They went away, leaving him with the sheriff, and strolled up to the general store, where they made a few purchases and were going back to their room, when the sheriff hailed them.

'This is a hell of a note!' he snorted. 'The prosecutor says that there's too much talk about the killin' of Joe Lane. He says that it ain't never been proved that Joe Lane was stealin' cows when Ludden killed him, so now he demands that I arrest Ludden.'

Hashknife whistled softly.

'Gee, that's too bad. But I can see his viewpoint, Sheriff. We all took Ludden's word for it.'

'I s'pose that's true, Hartley, but I hate this job of mine! Oh, well, I suppose if I arrest enough of 'em, I'll get the guilty ones after a while. This damn' prosecutor will bring a charge of murder against old Hank, as sure as hell. He ain't got no heart, liver, or lights when it comes to makin' a case against somebody.'

'They're all alike,' said Hashknife sadly. 'I like to settle all my cases out of court.'

'Yeah, I hear yuh do,' meaningly. The sheriff sighed deeply. 'Well, I s'pose that's the best way. But I've got my orders, and I've got to do it. Old Armadillo will prob'ly hit me with the grindstone or a two-faced axe before I can get Hank off the ranch. It sure is Hard Luck Ranch.'

Much against his will the sheriff rode away to arrest Hank Ludden. Sleepy and Hashknife went to their room and sprawled on the bed, where Hashknife smoked innumerable cigarettes and ignored all of Sleepy's questions.

'Thinkin', eh?' Thus Sleepy indignantly. 'Well, there's sure a-plenty to think about. By golly, I could almost set down and do some thinkin' myself—almost. Rotten deal for Ludden. He never killed Joe Lane on purpose. This'll set a fine example for the rest of the rustlers.

'Pretty soon a sheriff will have to take out a licence as an executioner in order to compete with crime. Hank Ludden up and shoots a cow-thief instead of kissin' him, and they throw Ludden in jail. By golly, I'm sure goin' to set on my gun-hand in this country.'

'How in hell can yuh expect a feller to think?' demanded Hashknife indignantly. 'You sure do flow vocally, pardner. Ho, hum-m!'

Hashknife sat up on the bed and dusted the tobacco from the folds of his shirt.

'Conscious again, eh?' grunted Sleepy. 'I suppose you've got it all figured out now, and all we've got to do is to go out and put the handcuffs on the criminals. My golly, yuh sure do go in a trance, tall feller.'

'I ain't got it all clear yet,' grinned Hashknife.

'Have yuh got any of it clear?'

'Clear enough for me, but not enough for a jury. They need a lot of facts, while all I need is a hunch. It's too stuffy up here, so I'll play yuh a game of pool. I need somethin' to take my mind off the troubles of the world.'

They left their room and went across the street to the War Paint. All was serene in Arapaho City, drowsing beneath a warm sun. Only two or three men loafed in the saloon, and the bartender sprawled across the bar, reading a love story. Hashknife and Sleepy went to the rear of the room and began playing pool. It was one form of relaxation that appealed to Hashknife, who was able to banish all else from his mind in the serious business of trying to figure out bank and combination shot. Neither of them was a good player.

They were in the midst of their string of fifty markers when Dayne of the Five Box came clattering in, the rowels of his big spurs jangling over the rough floor.

'Does anybody know where the doctor is?' he asked loudly.

Hashknife and Sleepy stopped playing, while the rest of the men in the saloon denied all knowledge of the doctor's whereabouts.

'Somebody sick?' asked the bartender, marking the place in his paper-backed novel.

'Aw, that damn'-fool cattle buyer got

himself killed, I think. I've got to get the doctor to pass judgment, though.'

'Amos Hardy killed?' The bartender was shocked.

'I think so.' Dayne leaned on the bar, bracing himself with his crooked elbow.

He rubbed his broken nose and squinted at Hashknife and Sleepy, who came up to the bar, still carrying their cues.

'How did it happen?' asked Hashknife.

''Bout a mile this side of the ranch.' Dayne spat dryly. 'Hardy was drunk. He wanted to drive, but Corliss wouldn't let him. They had quite a quarrel, so Corliss says, and when they was goin' around a turn in Sweet-water Canyon, Hardy grabbed the whip and slashed the team with it.

'That team wasn't more'n half broke, yuh know. Corliss tried to hold 'em, but he broke a line, the right one, and throwed all the pull on the left. Corless jumped, and all he got was a skinned leg. It's about forty feet straight down to the bottom, and all rocks. One horse was killed and we had to shoot the other. O'Day told me to get the doctor out there as soon as I could, but I can't find him. Don't reckon it'll do Hardy any good, 'cause he's too dead to skin.'

One of the men reported that he had seen the doctor go into the general store across the street, and Dayne left his interested audience to hurry to the store. Hashknife and Sleepy went back to their unfinished game, but did not complete it.

They had known Amos Hardy for a long time, and his death had taken away their desire to play pool. Dayne found the doctor at the store and they went away together.

It was about two hours later that the sheriff came back to town, bringing Hank Ludden, and accompanied by Armadillo Jones, who was mad enough to fight the world. Ludden was lodged in a cell across the hall from McLeod, and the sheriff and Armadillo were back in the office when Hashknife and Sleepy came and told them what had happened to Amos Hardy.

The sheriff threw up both hands.

'What next?' he wailed. 'By grab, I'm sick of all this trouble!'

'You and me both!' snorted Armadillo. 'Lemme git my hands on that damn' prosecutin' attorney. I voted for that polecat. Actually did. Thought he had brains. Arrestin' old Hank! My God, the old man is grievin' his heart out over killin' Joe Lane, and now a fool of a lawyer has him arrested.'

'Well, I can't help it!' snapped the sheriff. 'It wasn't my idea, Armadillo.'

'Nobody blamin' yuh, is there? I voted for you, too.'

'Yeah, and if yuh think I'm thankin' yuh for that vote, you've got another think comin',' retorted the sheriff. 'If I ever run for this damn' office, I hope I don't get a vote.'

'Yuh prob'ly won't,' said Armadillo, and added dryly, 'not if I have anythin' to say about it.'

Hashknife and Sleepy grinned at the repartee. It was like a little terrier snapping at the heels of a Great Dane. They were the best of friends, but both of them were so exasperated that they used each other as an outlet.

'I'm goin' up to see Mary Lane,' declared Armadillo. 'I'm goin' to gird up my loins and tell her who's which.'

'It won't do yuh no good to wish more trouble on her,' said the sheriff. 'She'll find out, anyway.'

'Of course she will. But I want her to know jist how her daddy feels about the shootin'. It'd make a lot of difference to Hank if Mary would come down and see him. That old fool would set right there and let yuh hang him, 'cause he thinks there ain't nothin' left in the world.'

'Well, she won't never come,' declared the sheriff.

Armadillo squinted closely at the sheriff. 'You won't do anythin' to stop her if she wants to come, will yuh?'

'Of course not.'

'All right.' Armadillo spat violently, hitched up his belt, and went bowlegging his way out of the office.

It was not a job to Armadillo's liking, but he knew it must be done. He had really wanted an excuse to talk with Mary. Somehow he could not believe that Mary would refuse to see her father. At least, he thought she would not refuse to see him.

He turned the corner at the old cottonwood and went out to Lane's house, a little one-story, unpainted cottage. There was little style to the Arapaho residential architecture. The front yard was enclosed with a picket-fence, many pickets being missing, and the gate sagged from one hinge.

It creaked loudly when Armadillo opened it, and he looked apprehensively towards the house. Nothing happened.

There were a few rose bushes in the front yard, and Armadillo stopped to examine them, for no reason except that it delayed him.

He heard the front door open, but did not look up. Another bush drew his immediate attention. Finally he lifted his head and looked at Mary Lane, standing just outside the door. For several moments they looked at each other. They might have been total strangers, as far as recognition was concerned.

Armadillo looked back towards town, removing his hat and rubbing the side of his head with heel of the same hand. He turned back and looked at Mary.

'What do you want?' she asked softly.

'I had to come, Mary,' he said simply. 'They said yuh wouldn't have anythin' to do with us any more, but I'—he smiled slowly—'yuh know I never was any hand to believe what I heard.'

'Oh, I never said such a thing, Armadillo. But after what happened, you—'

'Oh, I *sabe* all that. It sure was an awful blow. It almost killed Hank Ludden, too.'

Mary's lips shut tightly and she looked away.

'It made him a hundred years old, Mary.

He'd give his life to bring Joe Lane back. We was a pair of old fools, Mary. We was jealous of Joe Lane, I reckon. We didn't realize that both of yuh was young.'

'But it's too late now,' she said painfully. 'I'm sorry about Dad. I might have been wrong, too.'

'Yeah, it sure looks like it was too late, Mary. Yore dad was arrested to-day for the killin' of Joe.'

'What?' Mary came closer to Armadillo, searching his face, wondering if she had misunderstood.

'Yeah, it's true, Mary,' he said slowly. 'He's in jail. The prosecutin' attorney made the sheriff do it. He said that there was no proof that yore dad had shot Joe while Joe was in the act of stealin' cattle. They'll give Hank a hearin' to-morrow, 'cause court opens the next day.'

'But they don't think that Dad did it—' Mary hesitated, shaking her head, her eyes wide. 'Armadillo, do they think that Dad lied?'

'That's what they think, Mary. But they're crazy.'

'Then you think Joe was a thief?'

'Aw-w-w, hell!' Armadillo floundered badly. 'I don't know what I think, Mary.

I've talked it over with yore dad until I dunno whether I'm afoot or on horseback. I wanted to be the one to tell yuh. Yore dad is settin' down there in the jail, lookin' at the wall, wonderin' what'll come next. I told him I was goin' to see yuh, and he said it wouldn't help any, but for me to tell yuh he was sorry.'

'Sorry, Armadillo?'

'Well, that's about all he could tell me. Hank never was a good hand at expressin' himself except with profanity. Bein' sorry means a lot for him to admit, Mary.'

'But what can I do?' asked Mary helplessly.

'Go down and talk with him, girl. He's yore dad. Stick to him. He didn't hurt yuh on purpose, honest he didn't.'

'I don't believe he did,' she said slowly. 'It hurt me so much that I haven't been able to think.'

'I'll betcha that's right, Mary. It sure was tough. I jist wondered how yuh was gettin' along for money, yuh know.'

'Oh, that part of it is all right, Armadillo. The county is going to pay me—'

She hesitated. The sheriff had told her not to talk about it.

'Yeah, I heard they was,' said Armadillo

with great satisfaction.

He wondered how the sheriff had fixed it up. Mary looked at him, wondering how much he knew. If he had heard of the generosity of the county, it was no longer a secret.

'Yes,' she said, 'it is wonderful. It seems that they don't believe Joe was dishonest, because they are going to pay me three times what Joe's salary would have been. Just think of it! Three hundred and thirty dollars a month!'

Armadillo gulped heavily, blinking his eyes. Three hundred and thirty a month!

'But please don't mention it to any one, Armadillo. The sheriff said the county didn't want it generally known.'

'I sh'd think not,' muttered Armadillo blankly.

Mary got her hat and accompanied Armadillo down to the jail, where they found Hashknife in charge, the sheriff having gone to the Five Box Ranch.

Hashknife shook hands with Mary, although he had never been introduced, and offered them chairs.

'I'm runnin' this place right now,' smiled Hashknife as he closed the front door and locked it.

He took a key from the sheriff's desk and walked to the door which connected the office with the jail.

'I'll let my star prisoner come out here to yuh,' he told them. 'The key will be in the lock, and when yuh get through talkin' yuh can lock him in again. This may not be accordin' to Hoyle, but there's a lot of things done around here that ain't accordin' to Hoyle.'

He walked back to Ludden's cell, swung the door open, and told Ludden he was wanted in the office. Wonderingly the old man headed through the doorway, while Hashknife closed the connecting door and went quietly out the rear.

Hashknife had no fear of Hank Ludden's escaping, and he did not want the meeting of father and daughter to occur in the presence of McLeod. Not that it would make any difference, except that Hashknife had an idea that it might better be held in private.

He went to the War Paint, where he joined Sleepy. Several more cattlemen had ridden in and were discussing Hank Ludden's arrest and the death of Amos Hardy, who was well known. None of them were in sympathy with the law regarding the arrest of Ludden.

They were willing to take it for granted that Hank had shot Joe Lane for rustling cattle, and they indignantly wanted to know what they were to do in case they caught a rustler red-handed.

'Git up a petition orderin' him to leave the country,' decided a bandy-legged cowboy seriously. 'Or yuh might speak severely to him.'

'And git arrested for slander,' grunted another, which caused a general laugh.

It was a short time later that the sheriff and doctor came back with the body of Amos Hardy, which was left at the doctor's office. Hashknife joined the sheriff, and they were almost to the office when Mary and Armadillo came out. 'I left 'em alone to talk with Hank,' explained Hashknife.

'Tha's all right,' said the sheriff. Mary greeted him with a smile and a handshake.

'I hope yuh ain't sore at me, Mary,' he said.

She shook her head quickly.

'Not a bit. It isn't anything you could help.'

'I'm sure glad yuh feel thataway. Come again.'

'I surely will.'

They went on, and the sheriff looked quizzically at Hashknife, who shrugged his shoulders.

'Armadillo brought her,' he said. 'I'm glad for Ludden's sake.'

'So am I.'

They went into the office and sat down. The sheriff stretched wearily, his big hands dropping loosely in his lap, while his sad eyes contemplated the opposite wall.

'Hardy was dead, eh?' queried Hashknife.

'Yeah. Musta landed down in that canyon on his head. The team and buckboard are still there. Too much liquor.'

The sheriff took a bundle of papers from his pocket and placed them on his desk. From another he took a sum of money, a pocket-knife, a watch.

'Amos Hardy's personal effects,' he said sadly.

'Mind if I look at 'em?' asked Hashknife.

'Certainly not. Go ahead.'

Hashknife examined all the papers, which consisted of some personal letters, business letters, telegrams, business cards. He looked them all over carefully and put them back.

'We've got to send word to his firm,' said the sheriff. 'Nobody around here knows where Hardy's home is.'

'I never heard,' said Hashknife thoughtfully. 'When do yuh give Hank Ludden a hearin'?'

'To-morrow mornin'. Court opens the next day, and we've got to find out if Hank has got to stand trial. There ain't a lot of cases on the calendar, and we can't hold Hank Ludden for another three months.'

'I don't see how they can hold him,' mused Hashknife. 'He says Joe Lane was stealin' cattle. How can the law prove that Joe wasn't? It looks to me like a foolish case.'

'I reckon so, Hartley. But there's so much talk about it that the prosecutor has got to do somethin'. Old Hank won't hire a lawyer.'

'Prob'ly don't realize what it means. I'm naturally interested, because I told him I'd try and change the luck of the HL Ranch.'

'You've got a job, Hartley.'

Hashknife smiled softly and rubbed his nose. 'I did have,' he said slowly. 'See yuh later.'

He left the office and the sheriff squinted after him.

'He did have,' muttered the sheriff. 'Did have eh? Now what did he mean by that, I wonder?'

Hashknife's words were food for thought, and the sheriff of Arapaho tried to digest them. What did Hashknife know that the rest of them did not know, he wondered? Was he bluffing or did he really know something?

'I don't think he's bluffing,' decided the sheriff. 'That long, lean, question-eyed whippoorwill has seen somethin'. He's got a reputation that he didn't get from settin' still.'

Hashknife went up the street, and was standing in the doorway of the general store when Honey Moon and Dayne rode in and tied their horses at the War Paint hitch-rack. They waved at Hashknife as they went to the saloon—Honey Moon waddling along like a duck while Dayne went stiffly, his crippled arm giving him a peculiar appearance.

Some more cowboys came up the other side of the street and went into the saloon. Hashknife puffed on a cigarette, his eyes half-closed, as he tried to map out his next move. The cigarette burned his lip, and he spat it out.

Across the street he went, and into the War Paint. Sleepy was at the bar with the rest of the cowboys, and the conversation was still about the arrest of Hank Ludden. The Five Box boys were anxious to hear all about it, and the bartender, acting in the capacity of a town crier, was giving them plenty of information.

'Aw, that's a rotten deal,' declared Honey Moon. 'They can't never cinch the old man.'

'The hell they can't!' Thus the bartender. 'The law can cinch anybody. They could cinch me or they could cinch you. You ain't got a chance agin' a smart lawyer.'

'Yeah, and they'll get you, too,' said Sleepy seriously. 'Don't yuh know it's a crime to serve the kind of liquor you do? I've heard that you bought that barrel of whisky seven years ago, used out of it steady ever since, and you've still got two-thirds of it left.'

Sleepy hadn't heard any such thing, but he delighted in an argument. Before the spluttering bartender could frame a fitting defence, Hashknife came in beside Sleepy and offered to buy a drink. The acceptance was unanimous.

'You were talkin' about Hank Ludden,' reminded Hashknife. 'Didja ever stop to think what a conviction of him would mean to things out in the ranges?'

'Sure thing,' nodded Honey Moon. 'It'll mean that a man will be scared to shoot at a rustler unless he has a couple of lawyers along with him and a permit from the court.'

'That's just what it'll mean, Moon. Now, here's what we've got to do, boys. The case is awful weak on both sides, but we can't take any chances. Every one of you fellers bring in all the punchers yuh can. By golly, we can sure make it so uncomfortable for the law that they won't dare hold him. *Sabe?*'

'We'll sure do that,' said Honey. 'There's too danged much law around here, anyway.'

They drank to success. Hashknife's scheme appealed to all of them, and Hashknife drew Moon aside.

'Have O'Day come in, too, will yuh? He can protest just as hard as the rest of us, and the fact that he took the trouble to come down here will kinda add power to us.'

'I'll tell him,' grinned Moon. 'Yuh never

can figure out what Dutch O'Day will do. He thinks yo're a little tin god, Hartley.'

'I am,' said Hashknife seriously.

'Oh, yeah?' Moon's fat face expressed only a blank stare.

He didn't know whether Hashknife was serious of not.

'I'm pretty smart,' said Hashknife. 'Prob'ly a lot smarter than most folks, but I can't help it. I was born thataway.'

'Uh-huh,' Moon nodded foolishly. 'Well, I'd tell the boys.'

'Thank yuh.' Hashknife walked to the rear of the room and began practising on the pool-table, while Moon went back to the bar, wondering what kind of an egotistical fool Hashknife really was.

All the wonderful stories he had heard of Hashknife's ability were immediately discounted. He nudged Sleepy and attracted his attention.

'What kind of a feller is yore pardner?' he asked.

'Hashknife?' Sleepy squinted sideways at Moon. 'I'll tell yuh the truth, Honey—he's about half-loco.'

'Honest?'

'Well'—Sleepy shrugged his shoulders— 'a feller wouldn't say that about his pardner if it wasn't true, would he?'

'Um-m-m-m.' Moon glanced at Hashknife thoughtfully. 'No, I don't reckon yuh would. But I've heard so much about him.'

'Oh, yeah?' Sleepy turned and looked at Hashknife before replying. 'That was quite awhile ago, Honey. He used to be good. Yeah, he sure used to be a dinger. But now?' Sleepy shook his head sadly.

'Told me he was a tin god,' whispered Moon.

Sleepy choked. In fact he strangled, and there were tears on his cheeks before he could swallow again.

'He thinks he is,' said Sleepy hoarsely. 'He's all right if yuh leave him alone.'

'Sure.'

Moon and Dayne left the saloon. Sleepy went back to Hashknife and they racked up the balls for a game.

'What was Honey Moon whisperin' to you about?' asked Hashknife.

Sleepy leaned on the table and laughed so hard he missed the cue ball.

'He thinks yo're crazy, Hashknife. Did you tell him you was a tin god?'

'I admitted that I was,' grinned Hashknife.

The grin vanished as he slowly chalked his cue, and his eyes looked sombrely towards the front of the room.

'I might be, at that, Sleepy. The Tin God of Twisted River, if I guess right.'

Sleepy straightened up and looked keenly at Hashknife.

'Is it almost time to say "when," cowboy?' he asked softly.

'Almost,' Hashknife nodded thoughtfully. 'I'm all set, pardner. Mebbe I'm wrong, but I can almost read what's written after certain names in the Big Book. It ain't plain yet, but plain enough.'

'I *sabe*,' said Sleepy seriously.

He knew that Hashknife's work had not been in vain, although Hashknife had given him no inkling of what he had found out. It was not like Hashknife to tell any one what he was doing, and Sleepy had learned to follow blindly to the end.

'Do yuh know the name of the man who sent yuh the letter?' asked Sleepy.

Hashknife shook his head.

'Don't need it now.'

They stood for several moments looking at the layout of coloured balls and making no effort to continue play. Then Hashknife missed an easy side-pocket shot and dropped the cue ball in a corner pocket. Sleepy studied the layout for several moments, ignoring the fact that the cue ball was not in sight. All of which showed that their minds were not on the game. Then, as if by mutual consent, they put their cues in the rack and walked outside, where they sat down in the shade with their backs against the wall.

## CHAPTER ELEVEN

## ANSWER TO THE MYSTERY

That the cattlemen of Twisted River wished to keep their rights, so far as killing off rustlers was concerned, was attested by the fact that the ranges were well represented in Arapaho City the following morning.

The arrest of Hank Ludden was considered a direct slap in their faces, and a conviction would establish a dangerous precedent. So they had come to attend the hearing of Ludden and to protest vigorously.

Macey, the prosecuting attorney, had got

204

wind of Hashknife's scheme, met him at the sheriff's office and pointed out that he, Hashknife, was trying to interfere with the law.

'Nothin' of the kind,' laughed Hashknife.

'With the room filled with hostile cowboys, do you think a justice of the peace would dare decide against Ludden?'

'Well, you've got no case against him.'

'Very well. Then let the case decide itself. If we have no case against him, why bring all these cowboys?'

'Don'tcha like to act in front of a big crowd?' grinned Hashknife. Then seriously, 'Macey, I came here to find the answer to a mystery.'

'You did, eh?' The lawyer smiled indulgently. 'I don't believe in mysteries.'

'No, I s'pose not. Lotsa folks don't believe in Santa Claus, but they always get up early Christmas mornin' and take a good look around to see what has been left for 'em.'

The lawyer laughed. He had an exalted idea of his own importance, but he was just a trifle curious about the mystery.

'Just what mystery were you trying to solve?'

'You've heard of Hard Luck Ranch?'

'Yes. But as far as any mystery is concerned, no.'

'Perhaps it ain't no mystery to you when cattle disappear month after month and nobody knows where they went.'

The lawyer smiled.

'I've heard something of it. Perhaps there is a mystery in that. The other happenings were merely coincidences.'

'Certainly. I'm not tryin' to find out how it is that men get killed accidentally, and all that. That's none of our business. But losin' cattle, that's different.'

'I see. But what has that to do with the trial of Henry Ludden?'

'He killed a rustler, didn't he?'

'It seems to me,' said the lawyer solemnly, 'that we are not getting anywhere with our argument. I tried to point out to you the folly of trying to stampede my court with a lot of indignant cowboys, and you get me into an argument over some mystery.'

'Which shows that you ain't so awful narrow,' laughed Hashknife. Then seriously: 'Macey, here's the way your case stands right now. Hank Ludden ain't got any defence. He can't prove that any one was there, nor that a single head of cattle was in the corral. If you say that he met Joe Lane alone on the hills and killed him, he can't prove that you're wrong.

'Nor can you prove that yo're right. It's yore imagination against his word, and God knows what a jury might do. Do you want a conviction, whether the old man is guilty or not, or do you want justice done?'

The lawyer studied Hashknife for several moments.

'If you can prove it to my satisfaction— justice, of course.'

'Good. Now quit wailin' about the cowboys stampedin' yore courtroom. Forget the dignity of the court, and let me run part of the show to suit myself.'

'But you can't—' Macey started to protest, but the sheriff interrupted him.

'Let Hartley alone, Macey. I dunno his proposition, but I'm behind his play right now.'

'Well'—dubiously—'a court of law has a certain dignity to uphold, whether it is in a big city or on a cattle range.'

'It won't lose any dignity,' Hashknife smiled softly. 'See yuh later.'

Hashknife crossed to the War Paint, where a goodly crowd were already filled with good cheer. Honey Moon drew Hashknife aside and informed him that O'Day would be there soon.

Corliss, limping a little from his accident, shook hands with Hashknife.

'You got off lucky,' said Hashknife.

Corliss nodded quickly.

'I jumped just in time. How soon does that hearing start?'

'Pretty soon, I reckon. Get yore boys down close to the front where we can sort of look things over close, will yuh?'

'Sure thing.'

Hashknife motioned to the bartender, who came down to the end of the bar.

'Can I borrow that blackboard back by the pool table?' asked Hashknife.

The bartender squinted at the rear wall, where a blackboard, about three feet square, was suspended with a wire from a nail. It was used for keeping pool scores.

'Borrow it? Sure yuh can. But you'll bring it back, won't yuh?'

'Sure.' Hashknife lifted the wire off the nail, picked up a stick of chalk, and walked out through the back door carrying the blackboard, while the bartender squinted after him wonderingly.

'What is he goin' to do with the

208

blackboard?' asked Dayne, who had seen Hashknife depart.

'I could answer something else a lot easier than that,' grunted the bartender, and went back to his clamouring patrons.

Hashknife circled the saloon, crossed the street, and went into the building that was used as a courtroom. The door was open, but no one was in the room. There were a few benches, but most of the seats were chairs. A wide aisle down the centre was the only mode of inlet and exit.

The room was about fifty feet long and thirty feet wide, with a space of about fifteen feet deep railed off for the judge, jury, and those immediately concerned in the case. The judge's desk was an old roll-top affair on a level with the rest of the room.

Hashknife walked back to the desk and looked at the back wall. There were plenty of protruding nails on which to hang his blackboard. He selected one to the left of the desk which would allow the board to hang about five feet above the floor.

The blackboard was the same on both sides, and was scarred from much usage. Hashknife carefully drew some cabalistic marks on it, before hanging it, with the marks turned to the wall. Then he sat down on a front seat, rolled a cigarette, and waited for the time to come.

He had only been seated a few minutes when Sleepy came in. He sauntered down to Hashknife, squinting at the blackboard, and sat down.

'Goin' to do some examples for the class?' asked Sleepy.

Hashknife nodded.

'Dutch O'Day just drove in,' offered Sleepy. A noise at the door caused them to turn. The big Chinaman, How Long, was coming in, carrying O'Day.

'C'mon down here,' called Hashknife, and the Chinaman came grinning down the aisle, depositing O'Day on a front seat.

'Thank ye, How Long,' said O'Day, adjusting himself carefully. 'Ye may run down to the Pekin Café and enjoy yer old friend. I'll send for ye when this is over.'

How Long smiled and went shuffling out.

'Ye heard about Hardy, of course,' said O'Day. 'The poor devil. Too much liquor. Corliss tells me that Hardy was comin' out to pay me back for what I said to him,' O'Day sighed. 'Ah, it's true that when ye try to cook up a great heat against a man, ye may get scorched yerself. I know it, Hartley.

'They tell me that things may go against Hank Ludden. We've not spoken for two years, but I'd like to tell him that I'm for him.'

'He'd appreciate it, O'Day. His daughter was down to see him yesterday, and I hope things are right between them.'

'I hope so. She's a nice girl. I've seen her grow up, Hartley, but the other day was the first time I realized it.'

Men were beginning to drift in, and among them was Armadillo Jones, who came down to the front, selected his chair, and sat down defiantly. Hashknife noticed that Armadillo shifted his holster so that his gun rested across his lap. He glared at O'Day, but grinned at Hashknife and Sleepy.

The prosecuting attorney came in, carrying a book and some papers. He squinted at the blackboard, but said nothing. Armadillo's eyes followed every movement of the lawyer, and the little man's eyes were filled with hate.

The seats were filling rapidly, and the lawyer glanced at the crowd apprehensively. Finally he came to

Hashknife, speaking to him in whispers:

'I don't like the looks of this. If you have any influence over these men, I hope you will speak to them before the hearing begins.'

Harshknife nodded.

'I'll see that yore case ain't hurt.'

'Thank you.'

The three men from the Five Box came down the aisle, looking over the empty seats. There were twelve jury chairs at the left side, facing the judge's desk, and the three cowboys clattered over to take possession of three seats.

'My God, I'd hate to be on trial with a jury like that!' yelled a cowboy back in the crowd. It caused a general laugh, much to the embarrassment of the three cowboys, who did not realize that they were making themselves conspicuous. Honey Moon got up and opened the window near them. Someone clapped his hands in applause, and Honey Moon slipped back to his seat, wiping the perspiration from his brow.

Then came the sheriff, Hank Ludden, and Mary Lane. The roar of conversation ceased abruptly, and the last half of their walk to the table beside the judge's desk was made in silence. They sat down, and

Armadillo moved over to join them.

Ludden looked old and tired, but there was a smile in his eyes as he leaned over and listened to what Mary was saying. His long, grey hair was unkempt, and his big hands were locked together on the table, as he peered at the crowd beneath his heavy brows.

The justice who was to hear the case came bustling in. When not acting in his official capacity, he handled part of the affairs of the Arapaho-Casco stage line. He was too fat to be dignified and too unversed in court procedure even to be calm.

He wiped his brow, nodded to the prosecutor, and sat down heavily. From back in the room a man called:

'Remember, Hank, we're with yuh.'

Hank Ludden smiled. The prosecuting attorney shot a quick glance at Hashknife, who got to his feet, walked to the blackboard, where he printed in large letters:


ON THE OTHER SIDE OF THIS
BOARD IS THE ANSWER
TO THE TWISTED RIVER
MYSTERY

Then he put the chalk in his pocket and stepped aside. Every eye in the room was on the board, and from different parts of the room came droning voices as some read it aloud. The judge and prosecutor stared at the board and at Hashknife.

'Well, turn it over!' yelled an impatient cowboy, and the conversation roared again, as men asked each other what was meant.

'What's the mystery?' asked Corliss. 'Let us in on it.'

Hashknife leaned back against the wall and looked at the prosecutor.

'Mind if I talk a few minutes?' he asked.

'It looks as though you might have to talk,' said the prosecutor.

Hashknife grinned at the crowd.

'This little social gatherin' was for the purpose of seein' whether the law could try Hank Ludden for the murder of Joe Lane,' began Hashknife easily. 'The law didn't have no case, and Hank didn't have no defence.

'Now, I've got to go back a few months to a time when a man wrote me a letter from Arapaho City, warnin' me not to come and take charge of the HL Ranch. I didn't *sabe* it. Amos Hardy had told Hank Ludden to try and get me to come, and

214

gave Hank my address at Calumet.

'Hank's letter had a return address on it, so he got his letter back. The other letter had none, and that's why I got warned off a job I never took.'

Hashknife laughed softly and looked around. Every man was leaning forward, listening intently.

'So,' continued Hashknife, 'we came here to see why we wasn't wanted, and we ran into a killin'. We seen a man fall in the road, and a few minutes later Hank Ludden tried to kill the both of us. He thought we were the two men who had been with the one he had shot.

'But we got away, circled back to the road, and I think Hank chased us to town, where he got the sheriff and went out to find that he had shot his son-in-law. After we got away from Hank Ludden, another shot was fired, off to the west of us.

'But we got to town. The sun was in our eyes, and the horse and rider appeared so sudden-like and the horse went into the brush so quickly that we didn't see what colour it was.

'But'—Hashknife paused, scanning the crowd, as though trying to make up his mind what to say next—'I am goin' to

215

prove to you that Hank Ludden never killed Joe Lane!'

It was like dropping a bombshell in the room. For a moment there was silence, then a roar of wonderment, a laugh. Hank Ludden got to his feet; staring at Hashknife.

'Never killed him?' queried the sheriff. 'What do yuh mean?'

Hashknife held up his hand as a signal for silence. It was difficult to silence the room, but Hashknife waited.

'I am goin' to prove that Joe Lane was killed by the rustlers. Now keep still! I never got up here to answer questions.'

'Next thing, you'll be sayin' that McLeod didn't kill Naylor,' snorted one of the audience.

'He didn't!' Hashknife's reply snapped like a whip.

It left the audience goggle-eyed. They stared at him as if he had gone crazy. Hashknife's eyes flashed to the three Five Box cowboys and found them staring wide-eyed at him.

'Then who killed Naylor?' demanded a man on the second row.

'Hank Ludden!'

'For God's sake!' exclaimed a high-pitched voice. 'What'll he tell next?'

'What makes yuh think so?'

'How in hell could he?'

'Hank wasn't at McLeod's place!'

'Yo're crazy!'

The questions and arguments came too fast for any of them to be intelligible.

'Shut up!' The sheriff sprang to his feet and roared his order at the crowd. 'Set down! Now, keep still!'

Hashknife's lips grinned, but his eyes were as hard as flint as he waited, watching every movement. O'Day was staring up at him, his lips twitching, while Sleepy cautiously eased his gun loose in its scabbard, wondering what was coming next but ready for anything.

Ludden had not resumed his seat, but was leaning one hand on the table, staring at Hashknife, wondering if it could possibly be true. The sheriff's orders had caused the crowd to quiet enough for Hashknife to proceed.

'Hank Ludden saw three men at the old U6 corral,' said Hashknife. 'They were misbrandin' cattle. He shot one and the other two got away.

'Joe Lane, on his way to the Five Box, heard the shootin', and started towards it.

He ran into the two rustlers, who killed him, probably thinkin' he was workin' with Ludden.

'These rustlers knew that one of their bunch had been shot. They had to get him. For the sheriff to find him would be to incriminate all of them, so they substituted Joe Lane's body for that of their companion. Hank Ludden didn't know it, 'cause he never looked at it until the sheriff was with him.

'These two rustlers took the body of their companion with 'em. They had to alibi him, so they picked a fight with Scotty McLeod, to blame him and—'

Hashknife whirled, turned the blackboard around, disclosing a heavily chalked HL brand, with thin chalk lines added to it, which built it into a perfect Five Box brand.

The dénouement came so suddenly that Moon and Dayne were stricken dumb. But not so with Corliss, whose brains had worked out all these schemes for them. There were but two ways out of the room, the main aisle and the open window, and Corliss knew he could never make the window.

And, knowing that only a miracle could

save him, he was on his feet before the blackboard had completely turned, whipping out his gun as he came, fairly screaming an oath at Hashknife, who had drawn so swiftly that it was an even break between them; but Sleepy's six-shooter crashed out before either of them could shoot, and Corliss whirled sidewise, his gun falling to the floor.

Moon and Dayne dashed for the window, but Moon's grasp was inches short.

Both Hashknife and Sleepy were shooting at them, and at that distance there was little chance of a miss. Both Dayne and Moon were making a desperate effort to keep going. Dayne was partly shielded by Moon, who was more intent on escape than fight.

He whirled, falling with his back against the wall, and his one shot skittered along the table-top, filling old Armadillo's eyes with splinters. Dayne's gun clattered to the floor and he threw up his one good arm in a token of surrender, his two shots having gone wild; but he was surrendering to a higher power than the courts of law of Arapaho.

Hashknife vaulted across the body of

Corliss and drew Moon and Dayne apart. A look sufficed. He turned back to Corliss, who had managed to lift his head and was trying to speak. Hashknife held up his hand for silence, and the struggling crowd stopped long enough for Corliss to be heard.

'O'Day didn't know,' he said painfully, his eyes closed. 'It's all right. Moon said you was—a tin—god'

That was all. The courtroom quickly cleared, while the doctor went to work and the crowd waited outside for Hashknife. Two men carried O'Day to the edge of the sidewalk. He seemed too stunned even to ask questions, and his face was twisted painfully over the shock of it all.

★　　　★　　　★

Hank Ludden, Mary Lane, and Armadillo were inside a circle of men, who insisted on shaking their hands, and Hank Ludden hardly seemed to know what it was all about. The sheriff came from the courtroom and halted near Hashknife, who had come out just ahead of him.

'Hartley, how did you figure all that out?' he asked.

The crowd gathered around him, imploring him to tell them.

'I told most of it in there,' said Hashknife. 'There had to be a way to change the HL brand. It was awful simple to make it into a Five Box. I found out that O'Day was crippled and let Corliss handle his sales and all that. What could be easier than for Corliss to steal HL stock and sell 'em with O'Day's stuff?

'If I had known where to get in touch with Amos, I might 'a' checked up on his buying, and found out that he bought more Five Box cattle than O'Day got paid for, I reckon. But I wasn't so sure that O'Day wasn't mixed up in the stealin' from the HL.

'And when I did figure out that Corliss was the guilty party, Amos Hardy shows up and proceeds to get drunk and stick around with Corliss, so I had no chance to find out anythin'.

'Amos Hardy paid cash. O'Day got paid for his cattle, and Corliss, Naylor, Dayne, and Moon got paid for HL cattle. They tried to kill me and Sleepy at McCallville.

'Corliss was clever, but made the mistake of tryin' to kill us through a saloon window. They ruined the firin'-pins on the rifles we borrowed from the sheriff so as to cripple us for long-range work. They figured we'd ride back through Crow Rock Canyon in daylight and they could pick us off. And we might 'a' done it too, if they hadn't overplayed their hand by shootin' through the window.

'They put a note in McLeod's coat, feelin' that me or the sheriff would find it. It sent us to McCallville and almost got us killed.

'I wanted to be sure, and I couldn't feel sure until Hardy was killed. He said he had a list of every shipment he had ever bought from Dutch O'Day, and he was goin' to show it to O'Day yesterday. When the sheriff brought Hardy's effects back, that list was gone.

'Corliss killed Hardy to get that list. He couldn't afford to have O'Day know how many cattle had been shipped, because it would be a lot more than O'Day's list showed. So Corliss killed Hardy, took that list, and blamed the runaway.'

'But I knew nothin' about it.' O'Day's face twisted painfully. 'I didn't know it, lad.'

'I was sure yuh didn't, O'Day. If you had been guilty, Corliss would not have killed

Hardy.'

Hank Ludden came over to Hashknife, peering at him from beneath his shaggy brows.

'Hartley,' he said slowly. Just that. It was enough. Hashknife held out his hand and they gripped tightly.

'I'm glad I didn't get yore letter, Hank,' smiled Hashknife. 'It was written in the Big Book that the man who told you about me had to die first.'

'Yes,' said Ludden simply.

Mary did not speak, but the look in her eyes, as she gazed at Hashknife, was payment enough.

'Ah, I'm sorry,' muttered O'Day. 'Ludden, my men robbed ye for a long time. Put my brand on yer stock. Of this I had no knowledge, but ye'll not lose. I'll make good. It's about all there is left in life for me to make good.'

The tall, thin county treasurer pushed his way through the crowd and held out his hand to Mary Lane.

'Congratulations,' he blurted. 'The—I was just talking to one of the commissioners who was in there—in the courtroom. They have—er'—he winked boldly at Hank Ludden, who had given him the cheque to issue in monthly payments to Mary—'they have decided to go right on paying you—er—another one hundred and ten dollars per month.'

Mary looked at him blankly and at the sheriff, whose mouth was wide open like a fish out of water. Then the sheriff turned and went striding towards his office. It was too much for him. Hashknife and Sleepy overtook him before he reached the office, and he was talking to himself, something about four hundred and forty dollars per month, but did not explain to them.

'I'm goin' to turn McLeod loose,' he muttered. 'He'll sure be glad to have yuh tell him all about it.'

He swung open the door and stepped inside, but Hashknife and Sleepy kept right on going towards the livery stable.

Their room rent was all paid up and they had no baggage to get. Swiftly they saddled and rode out of Arapaho City, circling the town and going away the same way they had come.

The crowd was still in front of the courthouse, probably wondering what had become of Hashknife and Sleepy, but they were doing what they had done many times before—getting away ahead of thanks and hero worship.

They pounded across the Twisted River bridge and along the dusty road, passing the spot where Joe Lane's body had been found and drawing rein only when they saw the old sign—ARAPAHO CITY.

'This is a quitclaim deed for my share of the darned thing,' read Sleepy. He glanced sidewise at Hashknife. 'Shall we get off and sign it, cowboy?'

Hashknife shook his head slowly, looking back down the old road. 'No-o-o, I reckon not, Sleepy. Arapaho City and the Twisted River country is pretty good now.'

'Pagans,' said Sleepy seriously.

'What do yuh mean?'

Sleepy grinned and reached for the makings of a cigarette.

'Worshippin' a tin god,' he said.

Photoset, printed and bound in Great Britain by
REDWOOD BURN LIMITED, Trowbridge, Wiltshire

FTS

12/80  Bca  Wittle

wc
DB